COURAGE MOUNTAIN

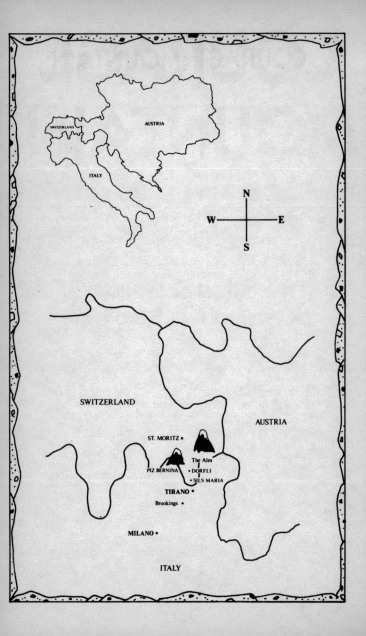

COURAGE
MOUNTAIN

The Further Adventures of Heidi

The official movie tie-in
by Fred and Mark Brogger

Published by The Trumpet Club
a division of Bantam Doubleday Dell Publishing Group, Inc.
666 Fifth Avenue, New York, New York 10103

ISBN: 0-440-84134-8

Reprinted by arrangement with Viking Penguin, a division of Penguin Books USA Inc.
Printed in the United States of America
January 1990

10 9 8 7 6 5 4 3 2 1

OPM

To Barbara, Christine, Greg, Karen and Walt,
who all learned to cross that mountain.

COURAGE MOUNTAIN

CHAPTER 1

High above the glistening Swiss Alps, a lone hawk soared and dipped through the brilliant sky. Twisting and gliding with effortless ease among the magnificent peaks, the hawk gradually began his descent. Below him was the village of Dörfli. Chaletlike houses resplendent in their colors of yellow, blue, and salmon pink gleamed brightly in the afternoon light. The hawk swooped low over the church steeple, the highest point in the village, just as the church bells began their call to evening worship and ended this October day in the year 1915. As the hawk swept up the Alm, the mountain above Dörfli, away from the sound of the bells, many of the hard-working people of the village began their walk to the church to offer their thanks and prayers. They were grateful that their country had so far been spared the horrors of the war raging on three of Switzerland's borders.

1

High up on the Alm, set on a massive shelf of rock, stood a large woodcutter's hut that overlooked the valley and Dörfli far below. It was built of stone and looked as if it could stand for hundreds of years braving the alpine winds and snow. Wildflowers grew everywhere.

The old man with the craggy, weathered face came down the narrow trail from the upper glacier and stopped, surveying the valley below him. As he gazed down at the Alm hut he had built with his own hands, he reflected on the happiness that had come to him when his granddaughter, Heidi, had first arrived on the Alm several years before. Once he had been a bitter recluse sitting high on a mountain, hating everyone and everything. Heidi had shown him how to once again open his heart. A deep sigh escaped him as he thought of Heidi leaving the Alm, for tomorrow she was expected to board the train for Italy and a new world: The Brookings Academy for Girls, a distinguished private boarding school in Tirano that Heidi's cousin, Klara, and her family in Frankfurt had arranged.

The old man winced as he thought of Heidi in a private girls' school. It would be so strange for her. He knew she didn't want to go away, but he persisted in having Heidi at least consider the opportunity of such an education. Yet, he had told her it must be her decision; he certainly was not going to force her to go. The hawk circled above Grandfather's head and cried out softly. It was as if the Alm hawk was trying to reassure him that Heidi would make the right decision. The old man smiled; he understood. He waved to the hawk and continued down the trail toward the hut.

Inside the Alm hut, Heidi was absorbed in a letter from The Brookings Academy for Girls which detailed what she could bring with her. She was seated on a small chair, Heidi's chair. On the cleanly swept wooden floor rested an open cloth valise half filled with clothes. Beside the valise, Heidi's white pet goat, Schwanli, eyed the valise suspiciously, having a premonition that the thing before him meant her mistress was going away. Schwanli looked up at Heidi with this question reflected in her soft brown eyes. But there was no response; her mistress was still looking at the piece of paper. Schwanli nuzzled her hand. Heidi lifted her head and smiled.

"It says here, 'three petticoats, three nightgowns, five pairs of cotton leggings, and you may wish to bring your diary or a favorite toy or book.' Schwanli, there just isn't room for everything."

Heidi, still holding the letter, got up from her chair and pulled from the valise her old rag doll and her wooden tea set. "They have so many things you must take; things I don't have. I can only bring with me what is on this silly list . . . not what I want to bring." She indicated to Schwanli the rag doll and tea set.

Annoyed, Heidi moved across the large room, which contained a large wooden table, a hearth, and her grandfather's bed off in one corner, to the simple stairs that led to her loft. At one time, when Heidi had first come to the Alm, there was only a rickety ladder. However, as Heidi grew older, Grandfather had carefully crafted the sturdier wooden stairs. As Heidi climbed the stairs, Schwanli decided she would investigate what was in the valise.

The hay loft, which served as Heidi's bedroom, was

3

directly under the eaves of the hut. One of Heidi's chores was to change the hay every morning so that it was always fresh and sweet-smelling. Heidi deposited the tea set and her rag doll in the small cupboard, saying good-bye to her childhood toys. The loft was Heidi's magical place. From the round window next to her bed she could see all the way down the valley to Dörfli. This was what she was going to miss the most—well, next to Grandfather, Heidi thought. Her loft with the magic window was her dreaming place and where she brought the books Klara sent her.

She looked at the Brookings letter. "What will it be like?" Heidi wondered. The idea of learning fascinated her, and she had always done well at the small village school. But that was over now, and she was hungry to experience new things and ideas. Heidi knew she should think of Brookings as a new adventure; that was what Grandfather said. Deep in her heart, Heidi knew he was right.

Grandfather didn't call her his little girl anymore, but instead, his young lady. Heidi thought about that for a moment. She had read enough books to know about men and women; how they fell in love and one day married.

"I suppose young ladies should go to boarding school, and after all, I am fourteen," Heidi said aloud. Nodding her head, she opened the Brookings letter and consulted the list.

" 'Each Brookings girl should bring a spare blanket in case of unreasonable chill,' " Heidi read aloud. She looked at the eiderdown that covered her straw bed. Shaking her head, she knew it would be impossible to get it into the valise. Nevertheless, Heidi gathered up the comforter and started down the stairs. Schwanli stopped when she saw Heidi. Her few clothes were scattered across the room.

"Schwanli!" Heidi yelled. Schwanli responded like any loved pet when screamed at. She ran for her life through the open door, still clutching Heidi's only flannel nightgown in her mouth. "You stupid old goat, bring that back," Heidi cried after him. Dropping the eiderdown, Heidi ran after Schwanli.

Grandfather looked up from his usual afternoon chore of chopping firewood, and laughed as Schwanli dodged back and forth to avoid Heidi. Now, it was a game. "Help me, Grandfather," Heidi pleaded. However, this was easier said than done as the fleet little goat gave both Heidi and Grandfather a merry chase before she was cornered. Heidi examined her nightgown.

"I don't think Schwanli wants me to leave. She took my things out of my valise and scattered them all over the floor."

Grandfather smiled. "I think she just wanted to play. Why don't you take her up to the glacier and collect Peter? I imagine that will give Schwanli all the exercise she will need for one day."

Heidi brightened at the thought of seeing Peter, but then remembered her packing. "I'd love to, Grandfather, but I have so much to do." Heidi glowered at Schwanli.

"I'll take care of that. Besides, you won't see the glacier

for some time now. . . . That is, if you're still leaving tomorrow?"

Heidi studied her grandfather's face, which as usual gave away nothing.

"I don't think I can go to Brookings. The silly list says I must have a blanket, but my eiderdown won't fit in my valise."

"You may have my blanket," Grandfather replied.

"But you'll freeze!"

"Nonsense," Grandfather gently replied. "Heidi, have you made a decision?"

"You mean about going to the glacier?"

"No. . . . Brookings," Grandfather said patiently. "Heidi, the money from Klara's family is a gift, not a punishment. I suggested using it for your education because I want you to be capable of providing for yourself, no matter what happens. You understand that don't you?"

"Yes, Grandfather," Heidi managed to reply, now somewhat downcast.

"But, I don't want you to go to Brookings just to please me. Otherwise you'll be saying to yourself, my cruel old grandfather made me come here." Heidi couldn't help but smile. "And then your time at Brookings will be wasted, and you'll have broken poor Schwanli's heart for nothing." A smile broke out on Grandfather's craggy face. He motioned to Heidi, who flew into his massive arms. Grandfather stroked her hair.

"Go, or stay, but you must decide . . . here." He gestured to his heart. "And whatever your decision, I will

6

understand and nothing more will be said. Now, no more lectures. Go and find Peter."

Heidi reached up and kissed her grandfather. "I love you," she said.

Although Grandfather was very moved, his face betrayed nothing. He pointed up the Alm toward the glacier. "Go!" he said, giving Heidi a playful push. The old man watched Heidi as she flew up the mountain trail with Schwanli in close pursuit; then he slowly, methodically, returned to the task of splitting logs.

The sun was beginning to set, deepening the vivid autumn colors of the high Alm as Heidi and Schwanli approached the glacier. She stopped to catch her breath, for it was a difficult climb. Heidi scanned the glacier for Peter and the small herd of goats he brought from Dörfli every morning to feed on the tender alpine meadow grass. However, there was no sign of either Peter or the village goats. She threw her head back and attempted to make the hawk call that Peter had tried to teach her when she had first come to Dörfli. She had never been able to get it quite right. According to Peter, her call sounded more like that of a wounded chicken than the noble alpine hawk. Nevertheless, Peter's answering call came moments later.

Heidi found Peter and his herd of goats in a small meadow near the top of the mountain. Peter waved as Heidi and Schwanli ran toward him through a sea of alpine flowers. She collapsed next to Peter while Schwanli went to join her grazing cousins.

"I never knew you came this high," Heidi said breathlessly. Peter laughed. Now eighteen, tall and athletic, and very much a young man, Peter rumpled Heidi's hair.

"Stop that!" Heidi cried. "You know I can't stand it when you do that."

Heidi grabbed a handful of wildflowers and threw them at Peter. Covered in flowers, Peter threw himself at Heidi. As when they were much younger, the two twisted and rolled in the sweet meadow grass, wrestling to see who would be the first to pin the other's arms. Usually Peter would let Heidi win, but not today. Laughing, Peter easily pinned Heidi's arms to the ground.

"Give up?" Peter teased.

"Get off me, you big oaf. . . . Peter!" Heidi squirmed and tried to push Peter away from her, but he was far too strong.

"No. I won't let you up unless you promise me you're not going off to that fancy school in Italy."

"You're just afraid that one day I'll know more than you," Heidi answered.

"With all those books you read, you probably do already. Anyway, I have a secret. . . ."

"Oh, Peter, tell me . . . please," Heidi pleaded.

"You're going to that school, aren't you?" Heidi looked up into his face and suddenly felt strange, almost weak in her stomach. What was she going to do without him?

"Well, are you?" Peter asked. Heidi slowly nodded her head. "I thought you might, so I joined the army."

"You did what? The army?"

Peter smiled, hoping that he had impressed his old friend. He reluctantly let go of Heidi's hands, realizing for the first time that Heidi was no longer a little girl. "I leave next week to begin my training," Peter said proudly.

Heidi still could not believe it. Everything was changing. "But, you can't . . ." Heidi protested.

"Why not? You're not the only one who can have an adventure, you know."

Feeling somewhat awkward, Peter slowly got up and extended his hand to Heidi. Heidi felt the strength in his hand as he pulled her to her feet. "You'll be a soldier . . . a man," Heidi said.

Peter was still holding on to her hand. "Silly, I'm already a man," Peter told her. Heidi looked up into his bronzed face and felt her knees go a little weak.

"If I promise not to go to Brookings, will you get out of the army?" Heidi asked.

"And how am I supposed to do that? I've joined for three years. Besides, I know you want to go that school and learn how to be a lady."

Heidi studied Peter's face carefully. "A lady? Do you think I'll ever become a lady, Peter?"

For a moment, he did not know what to say. He only looked down at her hand.

"Of course you will, and I'll come and visit you."

"You will? In your uniform?"

Peter nodded. "You know Tirano isn't very far," he said, pointing south to a towering peak. "It's really just the other side of the Piz Bernina."

As the sun set, Heidi and Peter stared off into the distance, both wondering what indeed was on the other side of that mountain. They were not even aware that they were still holding hands. They were on top of the world, in their own magical place where they wished time could stand still . . . maybe just for a little while.

Heidi lay in her straw loft bed with the eiderdown pulled up to her chin and looked out the window at the clear night sky. The soft sound of the firs bending to the gentle wind seemed to be whispering "We will miss you, Heidi." One small tear moved slowly down Heidi's cheek as she considered what tomorrow would bring. A new adventure, yes. But what would Brookings be like? Would the other girls like her? And could she truly bear to be away so long from the Alm and Grandfather? Once before, when she was only ten, Heidi had gone to Frankfurt to stay with her cousin Klara, but had to return to Dörfli after only a few weeks. Heidi brushed away the tear with an angry flick of her hand.

"Well, I was only ten then. My goodness, I'm not a baby. If other girls can do it, I certainly can. . . . Besides, I'm going to learn how to be a lady, and Peter will visit me in his uniform," Heidi said to herself. She imagined what Peter would look like in his army uniform, and thought back to how she had felt on the glacier only hours before: strange, but very nice in a way.

"Are you all right, Heidi?" Grandfather called out from his bed below.

"Yes, Grandfather. I was just thinking about tomorrow, but I'm fine, just fine," Heidi replied.

"Good. . . . Sleep well, my child."

"Good night, Grandfather."

The weather the next day was warm and bright, with hardly any wind. Heidi stood outside the Alm hut, drinking in the sights of her beloved Alm. She was dressed for travel in her one good dress and coat that Klara had sent from Frankfurt. Heidi much preferred her own clothes, but Klara had been quite insistent on how her cousin should look when she arrived at The Brookings Academy for Girls.

Grandfather emerged from the hut carrying Heidi's valise just as Schwanli grabbed hold of Heidi's new coat.

"Schwanli, no!" commanded Grandfather. The little white goat froze.

"I don't think she likes my new clothes, Grandfather."

"Nonsense, you look very nice . . . very grown up."

This perked Heidi up. "You really think so?"

Grandfather smiled and nodded. He carefully put the valise down and looked around him. "What a beautiful day," he remarked. Heidi and Grandfather looked down toward the valley and Dörfli in the distance. Then, Heidi turned for one final look at the high Alm and the glacier far above her.

"I wish I could take everything I see and carry it with me," Heidi said quietly.

"The Alm is inside you, my child . . . which is fortunate, as I don't think you could fit one more thing into this valise." They both laughed. But there was still something Grandfather wanted to say. He was not a man of many words, yet he knew it was his duty to say them.

"Heidi, I am happy that you made the decision to go

to the school. I know it wasn't easy for you, nor for me. Part of me wanted you to stay, but that would have been selfish." Heidi wanted to interrupt, but Grandfather held his hand up.

"As I have said, you have been given a wonderful opportunity, but you'll have to work especially hard, child. It will not be easy and it is going to seem strange at first. Most of your classmates will have come from wealthy families, far, far different from us. But I know you are strong and will endure these difficulties.

"Always remember, Heidi." Grandfather gestured toward the high Alm. "This is your strength; it will never desert you." Heidi's eyes were wet as she ran to Grandfather. He held her tightly to him. In the distance, they heard the sound of Peter's pan pipes. Grandfather brushed away Heidi's tears. "Come, it is time to join Peter. Say good-bye to Schwanli." Grandfather picked up the valise as Heidi knelt to give her goat a farewell hug. Then, grandfather and granddaughter started down the mountain.

Before long, Peter, very proud in his new army uniform, and Heidi were waving good-bye to Grandfather, who stood on the crest of a hill above them. The Alm hut and the glacier rose majestically behind him. Grandfather watched Peter pick up the valise and take Heidi's hand. She waved one last time, and then the two turned and continued down the Alm trail toward Dörfli. As he watched Heidi and Peter disappear from view, the old man sighed. He was going to miss her very much. Grandfather heard a cry, and looked up to find the alpine hawk circling above him.

"Yes, old friend, you came to say good-bye as well."

In Dörfli, Heidi and Peter made their way through the crowded square. It was market day, and the farmers were pushing their handcarts full of cheese and produce into the square. Others were setting up their displays of handicrafts, while women were bringing large baskets of fresh bread and cakes to sell. Several of the townspeople waved a greeting to Peter and Heidi. They were all quick to take note of Peter and his new uniform. He was so handsome, Heidi thought.

"I'm going to have a uniform too, a Brookings uniform! I'll bring it back with me at Christmas so you can see it," Heidi exclaimed.

"Christmas is for children. Do you think the army cares about Christmas? By then I'll be in some far-off land earning medals for valor," Peter teased.

Heidi grinned. "More likely demerits for bad conduct."

In front of the church was a small country carriage. The horse and driver made the trip twice a day from Dörfli to the train station in Sils Maria. An elderly couple was already in the carriage as Peter easily lifted Heidi's valise into the open cart. He turned back to Heidi and took her hands.

"You promised you would visit me. You will, won't you?" Heidi asked.

"As soon as I have my first leave, and enough money." Peter saw that the driver was anxious to leave, and helped Heidi into the carriage. He reached into his pocket, then handed Heidi his prized set of pan pipes. "Here, so you won't forget me at that fancy school."

Heidi gratefully accepted the pan pipes. She wanted to

13

CHAPTER 2

The train wound its way south through the alpine valley guarded by the majestic alps, the sentinels of Switzerland. Large cumulus clouds from the west, beautiful in design but dangerous in their intent, signaled an approaching storm and the eventual coming of winter. It would be a short autumn. The valley itself was still a lush green and reluctant to accept the coming of winter and its snowy mantle. Sensing the change of weather, lazy cows, with their bells gently clanging, moved from the higher pastures toward the shelter of the valley floor and the barns that would harbor them.

As the train sped past a small village, Heidi turned from the window and opened the straw basket that rested on the seat next to her. She carefully placed the worn napkin on her lap, then withdrew from the basket her lunch of black bread and cheese. Except for two young Italian soldiers across from her and an elderly couple a few seats back, the car was deserted. From the corner of her eye, Heidi noticed that one of the soldiers was staring at her with a slight smile on his face. Not quite knowing what to do, Heidi smiled back.

"Are you enjoying your lunch?" asked the soldier.

Flustered, Heidi could only nod, then turned to the window. She heard the two soldiers laugh and her face reddened.

"Leave her alone, Carlo. She's just a baby."

Heidi's hand tightened on the piece of bread. Her back was to the soldiers, but she wanted to turn and tell them that she wasn't a baby. She was going to Brookings and would become a proper young lady like the ones in the books Klara had sent her. Heidi could hear the soldiers whispering and she was sure they were talking about her. Well, she just wasn't going to cry and behave like a child. She righted herself in her seat and ever so carefully began to eat her lunch. Ignoring the soldiers and their obvious leers, Heidi forced herself to concentrate on the passing countryside and the Alps. Her mountains, Heidi thought, and the home she was leaving.

A military band was positioned to one side of the platform. The Tirano train station was crowded with people who had come to send off the many soldiers who would board the incoming train from Switzerland, bound for Milano and then east. There was a festive air as the band played, and the soldiers said good-bye to their loved ones.

Italy had entered the war on the side of Britain, France, and Russia when they had formally declared war on the Austro-Hungarian Empire five months before, but it wasn't until September that they had begun to mobilize. The Italian government and general staff had finally decided that they would concentrate their armies on the eastern front. One long whistle blast rose above the pomp and circumstance of the band, announcing the arrival of the awaited train.

As the train came to a stop in a cloud of steam, the band struck up another bright military air. The disembarking passengers were at first surprised at the platform reception, but then quickly became caught up with the gala occasion. As Heidi stepped down from the train, Carlo, one of the soldiers from her train compartment, offered to help her with her valise.

"Thank you, but I can manage," Heidi said with a polite smile as she marched past the two open-mouthed soldiers. With a twinkle in her eye, happy that she had put the two soldiers in their place, Heidi made her way down the crowded platform. With all the new and exciting sights and sounds, Heidi completely forgot that she was supposed to meet Mrs. Hillary from the school. There were a few whistles and winks from the soldiers as they started to board the train, but Heidi accepted it all with a smile. The bright hues of the flags and bunting, the wonderful Italian sounds and color, the embraces and the tearful farewells, the oompapah of the band—Heidi carefully absorbed it all. She almost pinched herself. "Is this really happening?" she said to herself. Picking her way through the crowd of soldiers was becoming more difficult, and Heidi finally had to put her valise down in order to get her bearings, as well as to rest her tired arm. An attractive soldier was beside her in moments and with a deep bow offered his help.

"May I be of assistance, *signorina?*" Heidi looked up into his smiling face, but before she could answer the band struck up a popular polka.

"Dance with her, Alberto," cried his friends. "Dance with her." They began to clap in time to the music and Alberto held out his hands to Heidi.

"Shall we?" he asked.

"But I don't know how," was all Heidi could say as she reached for his hands. And before she knew it, Heidi was dancing the polka. A wonderful dancer, Alberto whirled her up and down the platform with great expertise. Now everyone was clapping and cheering them on. Suddenly the band stopped playing and the train whistle pierced the air, announcing it was time to board. Noncommissioned officers shouted at the soldiers to get back in line.

Alberto took Heidi's valise to her. "*Buon giorno, signorina,* I must go. May I ask your name?"

"It's Heidi," she replied.

"Heidi . . . and I'm Alberto. Maybe the next time you hear a polka, you will remember me . . . yes?" Bending low, he gently kissed her hand and then was gone. Heidi watched him join his fellow soldiers, and just before Alberto boarded the train he turned and waved to Heidi. She waved back until she couldn't see him anymore, then reluctantly picked up her valise and once again started down the platform.

As she neared the station forecourt, Heidi noticed two children seated on one of the station benches. Thinking this must be some kind of official place for children to wait, Heidi suddenly remembered that she had been told in her letter she would definitely be met by somebody from Brookings. As Heidi neared the bench, one of the children, a girl in a tattered dress, turned and saw her. She touched the cardboard placard she was wearing around her neck, which spelled out the word ORPHAN.

"Are you an orphan, too? My name is Clarissa."

Heidi didn't quite know how to react but managed to say, "I have a grandfather."

"That's lucky. If I had a grandfather, I wouldn't be going to the orphanage."

Clarissa tapped the small boy next to her on the arm. All Heidi could remember afterward was that this child, who also wore a placard, was probably the dirtiest she had ever seen but also had the most wonderful large brown eyes. He smiled and pointed to her basket.

"He's Giovanni," Clarissa said, her eyes now also focused on Heidi's basket.

"Are you two hungry?" Heidi asked as she opened her basket. Her question was met with enthusiastic nods as Clarissa and Giovanni got up from the bench.

"Here, have some bread and cheese. I have plenty." Heidi handed the food to the grateful children, who could hardly refrain from gulping down the bread and cheese. As Heidi watched the two eating, she couldn't help but think: "Thank goodness I do have a grandfather." Suddenly over the roar of the crowded platform Heidi heard her name being called. "Heidi . . . Heidi!"

Heidi picked out an attractive woman in her early forties who was waving to her from the station entrance. This must be Mrs. Hillary, Heidi thought. She was dressed in a finely tailored Edwardian suit that carried a full-blown rose pinned to the lapel; next to her stood three girls of various ages, all dressed in the Brookings School uniform. Heidi noticed that Mrs. Hillary and her girls were having difficulty getting through the crowd, and when she stopped and signaled for Heidi to join them, Heidi turned back to Clarissa and Giovanni.

"I have to go now. But here, you can have what's left in the basket." As Heidi handed the basket to Clarissa and started toward Mrs. Hillary, Clarissa quickly grabbed hold of her skirt.

"What's your name?" asked Clarissa.

Heidi turned back to Clarissa, who looked up into Heidi's eyes, pleading for her to take them with her. "Heidi," she answered quietly. "I really have to go now."

"Can we come with you, Heidi? We don't want to go to the orphanage," Clarissa said.

Heidi hesitated only for a moment, then reached for Clarissa's hand and started toward the waiting Mrs. Hillary with Giovanni bringing up the rear. But suddenly she was facing a tall, very thin man, almost an apparition, dressed all in black, who was smiling down at her.

"These two little ones are with me." Startled, even somewhat frightened, Heidi could only hold on to Clarissa and Giovanni. "Forgive me, I didn't mean to startle you. I am Signor Bonelli, the director of the State Orphanage."

Mrs. Hillary, sensing Heidi's predicament, moved quickly to the rescue. She faced Signor Bonelli with all the hauteur at her command, motioning at the same time for Heidi to join her. "Mrs. Jane Hillary, headmistress of Brookings School, and you are detaining, sir, one of my new students." Signor Bonelli was most definitely amused, and presented Mrs. Hillary with a mocking bow.

"My apologies, of course, Mrs. Hillary. May I introduce myself, Signor Bonelli of the State Orphanage. It seems your new student was marching off with my two orphans . . . perhaps to enroll them at Brookings."

"Nonsense." Mrs. Hillary turned to Heidi and whispered, "You are Heidi, aren't you?"

"Yes, ma'am," Heidi answered.

"Very well, then. If you'll excuse us, Signor Bonelli." She started to lead Heidi off, but Clarissa was still holding on to Heidi's hand. With a swoop of his long arm, Signor Bonelli picked Clarissa up in one easy motion.

"Until we meet again, Mrs. Hillary . . . and Heidi, isn't it?"

Now holding Heidi firmly by the hand, Mrs. Hillary raised her significant chin to the appropriate angle and marched toward the station entrance. "We shouldn't talk to strangers, Heidi."

"They were hungry and were orphans." Heidi turned back for a moment and saw Clarissa wave as Signor Bonelli led her and Giovanni toward a side exit.

On reaching her waiting students at the entrance, Mrs. Hillary introduced Heidi. "Girls, this is our new student, Heidi. . . . And Heidi, this is Ilsa, and Gudron, and Ursula." The girls nodded, but before they could say anything Mrs. Hillary had set off for the main exit to the street.

As they made their way through the crowded station forecourt toward the exit, Mrs. Hillary, followed by Heidi and the three other girls, was chatting merrily away.

"We're a little sparse this year. Many of our girls were afraid to travel because of the hostilities. A shame, really; we're quite safe here in this part of Italy. They're sending all the troops to the eastern front, even though I doubt they do any fighting. The Italian soldier, dears, is not known for his fighting ability, but you'll find they have other qualities, *non è vero?*"

She glanced behind her to be certain the girls understood her meaning, and caught Ursula smiling at a young soldier. "Don't flirt with soldiers, Ursula, dear, it's vulgar." Except for Heidi, the girls giggled, knowing that Ursula was indeed a flirt. Since she was one of the few senior girls still at the school, Ursula was not that well liked by the younger girls, particularly Gudron and Ilsa. Ursula blushed at the reprimand, but then glared at the giggling girls; she would stand no nonsense from these two. As Heidi turned her head to see why Gudron and Ilsa were laughing, Ursula gave Heidi a look that spelled trouble.

Outside the street was jammed with horses and carriages waiting for the disembarking passengers now swarming out of the station. There were the usual curses from drivers as they attempted to move their reluctant horses into the street. Mrs. Hillary led Heidi and the girls down the narrow sidewalk toward a gleaming, open touring car. They marched right past Signor Bonelli, who had just finished depositing Clarissa and Giovanni into a black, hearselike carriage. He turned and saw Ursula as she went past and smiled.

"Ah," he thought, "this one is lovely." Signor Bonelli made a show of smelling a cake of scented soap he had pulled from his pocket. He presented the soap to Ursula. "For the *bella signorina*."

Ursula, completely taken by surprise, shrank back in fright. But Signor Bonelli, laughing, forced the cake of soap into her hand. He so enjoyed teasing these young things. He climbed into the carriage and signaled the driver, who with a flick of his lash sent the horses lurching forward. Ursula jumped out of the way just in time. Angry, she started to throw the cake of soap after the fast-moving carriage, but then changed her mind and instead concealed the soap in her jacket pocket. Looking ahead to make sure no one had seen what happened, Ursula hurried to catch up with the girls and Mrs. Hillary.

Heidi was in absolute awe of the shiny motor car, marveling at this giant machine and Mrs. Hillary's transformation as she donned the required duster. "Have you ever been in an automobile before?" Mrs. Hillary asked, at which Heidi could only shake her head. "Well, Heidi, a new experience already. Step up now, and girls, everyone aboard," Mrs. Hillary commanded. The other girls deferred to Ursula, who got in first as she was accustomed, but Heidi waited on the curb, not too sure about the whole thing.

There was a loud roar as Mrs. Hillary started the engine. Heidi jumped back. She would just as soon walk, thank you. Mrs. Hillary gestured to her to get in while the girls, led by Ursula, laughed. Heidi took a deep breath and climbed into the open automobile. Mrs. Hillary eased off on the clutch, and with a thump they were off. Horses shied at the horrific sound while people ran for their very lives as one horse and carriage bolted up the sidewalk, scattering luggage in every direction. Oblivious to the panic and confusion, Mrs. Hillary, her duster billowing about her, conscious of her historical role as the first woman in Tirano to drive a twelve-cylinder touring car, drove the new machine with gay abandon as it rattled and sputtered down the street. Now completely at ease with the puffs and groans coming from the internal-combustion engine, Heidi joined the other girls in waving to the frightened pedestrians.

The villas were so large, Heidi thought as they motored down the gravel country road. Tirano lay behind them and ahead was one beautiful villa after another. Heidi's mouth was wide open. She had never seen anything quite so grand.

"These are really quite pedestrian," Ursula commented, on noticing Heidi's admiration for the homes they passed. Heidi looked at her, not understanding. "I mean they are quite small, dumbkin. My home is at least twice the size of these and with much more land," Ursula proudly announced.

Ilsa screwed up her pretty little face; she had had just about enough of Ursula for one day. "So who cares about your stupid big house. It's probably filled with termites and rats." With almost royal disdain, Ursula turned away from Ilsa and Heidi and concentrated on the road ahead and the entrance to Brookings School.

24

Mrs. Hillary guided the gleaming automobile through the Brookings gates and started up the winding driveway, which was lined with elegant, tall pines. Through the trees, Heidi had her first glance of her future school and home. Once a magnificent mansion, Mediterranean in style, Brookings rose four stories from its finely sculptured lawns and gardens. Heidi's first thought, as the car pulled up in front of the entrance steps, was that the school seemed larger than all of Dörfli. Small girls in white play dresses were playing games on the front lawn, but stopped when they saw the car and ran over to greet the popular Mrs. Hillary. Ursula, Gudron, and Ilsa scrambled quickly out of the car to join their friends as Mrs. Hillary carefully dismounted. She looked at her only remaining passenger, who was still attempting to comprehend the size of the mansion.

Realizing what Heidi was experiencing, Mrs. Hillary smiled and extended her hand. "It's really quite cozy inside." Heidi slowly turned and looked at the kindly face of her headmistress. "Come, let me help you down, Heidi. Then I'll give you a private tour of your new home."

Heidi gratefully accepted Mrs. Hillary's hand and climbed out through the opened rear door. As the two started up the long front stairs, Heidi couldn't help but think of the Alm and Grandfather. Everything was so simple on the Alm. There she understood what was expected of her, and most of all it was where she was accepted and loved. All she could do was to hold Mrs. Hillary's hand that much tighter and swallow as they made their way up to the gigantic front doors.

CHAPTER 3

Heidi's first day at Brookings began very early. Just after sunrise, the girls assembled in the gardens behind the main house for their exercises. Heidi did not know what to wear for exercises. She decided on the flowered dress she had made herself. It was big and roomy. The other girls wore sailor-suit bloomers with big colored stripes on the tops—yet another outfit Heidi did not have.

The large gardens of the back lawn were meticulously cared for by the Brookings staff. Perfectly even green hedges surrounded the geometrically arranged flower plots. Heidi could tell that the flowers were saying their last good-byes as winter approached. The girls lined up in rows of four, yawning and rubbing the sleep from their eyes.

Mrs. Hillary, dressed also in exercise bloomers, wound

the crank and set the needle down on a phonograph on a table next to her. The sounds of violins and cellos filled the gardens.

"Girls, let us begin this morning with Mozart and our breathing exercise. Breathe in the morning and the music. It's the only way to start the day."

Heidi was in the front row, next to Ursula. She spread her arms out like Mrs. Hillary and began taking deep breaths. Heidi heard a giggle next to her as she tried her hardest at deep breaths.

"Breathe any harder and you'll blow up. Take ladylike breaths. Stand up straight," Ursula teased.

Heidi ignored the remark and tried to concentrate on the music. She had never seen a record machine before. The music seemed delivered by magic to the gardens. Heidi remembered Grandfather playing the organ in the church in Dörfli. His big hands floated over the keyboards, sending music out over the Alm. Grandfather had told her that music was his way of talking to the Alm.

Mrs. Hillary noticed Heidi staring at the phonograph. "Yes, the magic of the machine age, but we mustn't lose track! Listen to the music, Heidi. *Ascolta bene!* Let it lift your spirits. We're feathers. Feathers!"

The girls all laughed. They loved Mrs. Hillary, who was twirling about to the music at the front of the line. Trying to twirl like Mrs. Hillary, Ursula came crashing into Heidi. Annoyed and embarrassed, Ursula blamed the mishap on Heidi.

"We're feathers, not donkeys!"

Ilsa helped Heidi up. They both looked over at Ursula,

27

who paid no attention. Mrs. Hillary started the girls on their morning run about the grounds.

"Don't lag behind, lazybones," Ursula scolded as she hurried to catch up with Mrs. Hillary at the head of the group. Ilsa brushed off Heidi's dress and gave her a smile.

Heidi and Ilsa joined the group as they ran laps around the main house. Heidi looked at the mountains staring down at Brookings. The sun was getting stronger as it rose above Heidi's distant home. The other girls were panting heavily on the second pass of the house, but Heidi made the run with an easy stride. She was used to hiking up the Alm with its thin, clean air. Heidi pretended she was running on the high Alm with Peter. They were talking of the future. Would she be the wife of a heroic soldier who made his name in battle? Would he be the husband of an educated, refined, elegant lady?

"Heidi, daydreaming is not a productive method of exercise," Mrs. Hillary said as she broke into Heidi's thoughts of Peter and home. Heidi had fallen behind the rest of the girls.

"Sorry, Mrs. Hillary." Everyone else had gone into the main house for breakfast. Heidi followed Mrs. Hillary feeling slightly embarrassed.

The large dining room was filled with the boisterous chatter of hungry girls and the rattle of plates and fine silver. Two long tables were covered with platters of eggs and strudels and baskets of freshly baked rolls. Ursula sat at the head of her table, a seat she always grabbed for herself. As usual, she was schooling her younger classmates in manners. Ursula noticed Heidi looking in amazement at all the food in front of her.

"We pass our plates at breakfast. We're served only at night, here." She shoved a plate into Heidi's hands and continued. "At home we're served at every meal. Mother is quite proper."

Heidi looked around and thought everything was quite proper. Her cousin Klara lived in Frankfurt amid all the fineries one could wish for. Heidi had learned which silver to use, even when to use the little fork on her left. But Ursula was making her feel like a peasant. She took a crusty roll from the basket and split it open. A little wisp of steam escaped as she spread a big glob of red jam on the roll.

"No, no!" Ursula interrupted. "You break off the tiniest bit of bread and butter that. The rest you leave on your plate. You little Swiss cheese, don't you know anything?"

"Can't I eat all of it?" Heidi asked innocently.

Some of the girls around Ursula laughed, but Ilsa came to Heidi's rescue. "Don't pay attention to her, she's full of nonsense," Ilsa counseled.

"Excuse me, I didn't hear that," Ursula said in a superior tone of voice. Ilsa gave her a nasty look and popped a big piece of bread into her mouth. "These Swiss eating habits are contagious," Ursula said, moving to the other table in an effort to end the conversation.

"Is she always like this, Ilsa?" Heidi asked in exasperation.

"She thinks she is so grown-up. Just because she has— you know," Ilsa said, bringing her hands to her chest with a gesture that sent the rest of the girls into hysterics. Even Heidi had to laugh.

After breakfast, Heidi had class in the library. There were about ten girls seated at a large table with their writing tablets in front of them. Heidi marveled at the hundreds of leather volumes that lined the walls of the large wood-paneled room. Some of the books looked very delicate and old, but there was not a spot of dust on them. A new set of encyclopedias sat by the window that looked out onto the front grounds. These books must explain everything there was to know in the world, Heidi thought.

"Your essay for this morning will be titled Duty Determines Destiny. You are to defend or deny this truism," Mrs. Hillary told the girls as she walked around the table. She stopped by Heidi, who had turned around in her seat to look at the shelves.

"Do you like books, Heidi?"

"Oh, yes," Heidi beamed.

"A book is a great solace. A person can lose her family and fortune and suffer bitter disappointments in love— and still all is not lost, if one is surrounded by books. Often, I have turned to the comfort of reading when things seemed especially gloomy. There might be dark times ahead for the world, and knowledge will be our only salvation."

Heidi did not know what Mrs. Hillary meant, but she did love books. Klara had sent books to her over the years and she had read each of them several times. To Heidi, reading was not a chore to be done but a privilege to be savored. Not all young girls had stories to read.

"Heidi, you may take any book up to your bed at night.

I want every Brookings girl to be well-read. Leave a book closed on a shelf and it might as well not exist."

Heidi immediately pulled a book from the shelf, but Mrs. Hillary gently took it from her. "You have an essay to write, Heidi: 'Duty determines destiny.' "

Heidi turned back to the blank paper in front of her. Mrs. Hillary walked by her and put the book Heidi had chosen on the table next to her. "This is for later," she whispered. Heidi peeked at the book but returned to her essay.

"Duty determines destiny." She wondered what that meant. Her thoughts returned to Peter. He was a soldier now and had a duty to fight if the war moved into Switzerland. Duty, then, must be the responsibility to care for and protect things you love, like your country. But Heidi thought people would count as well. She would protect Grandfather if he were in danger. Or Peter. Or Mrs. Hillary. If they needed her in a time of crisis, she would do whatever she could to help them. That must be the destiny part, Heidi thought. She looked around at the rest of the girls, who were staring at their blank writing tablets. Heidi smiled to herself and began to write.

Heidi took her new book upstairs to bed with her. In the dormitory quarters, two rows of beds were lined up facing each other. At the foot of each bed was a small locker for clothes and personal items. Heidi's was filled with her few outfits and two books she had brought from home. Grandfather's big blanket covered Heidi's bed and draped down to the floor. Heidi opened the leather-bound book and carefully turned its delicate, yellowed pages. The printing was very antique and at the beginning of each chapter there was a drawing. Heidi looked at the first drawing, which was of the Greek god, Pan, half-man, half-goat. Pan was playing his pipes in a forest, calling the animals together. Heidi looked at Pan with his naked chest and goat's body. What a fanciful creature. Ilsa came over and looked at the picture with great fascination.

All of a sudden, Ursula noticed them looking at the drawing. "Don't look at that! Honestly, that's so disgusting."

"Don't be silly, Ursula," Ilsa said as she walked back to Ursula to finish the argument.

Gudron crawled up on Heidi's bed as Heidi put the book away so she wouldn't cause another commotion with Ursula. "That's the problem with Ursula, she's always shouting," Gudron said. "Heidi, do you live on a farm?"

"I live on the Alm," Heidi replied.

"But it's like a farm, right? You have pets, don't you?"

Heidi said, "We raise goats for milk and cheese. And we have two cows. My goat is named Schwanli. Grandfather and I—"

Gudron interrupted, determined to describe her own home. "I have a dog. Her name is Lady and she's an unusual color. She's blue."

Heidi looked bewildered. She had never heard of a blue dog and wondered if Gudron was making this up.

"You don't get that color too often, and she's a little crazy because whenever she runs out into the garden she turns three times and jumps up. She's also a bit scared of

other dogs and people, so she likes to sniff them like this."
Gudron made a loud sniffing noise. "I have to go to bed
now. Good night, Heidi."

Heidi was a little taken aback. Gudron could certainly
get excited when she was telling a story. She must miss
her home, Heidi thought. She picked up the writing set
that Klara had given her to write letters to her. She started
a letter to Grandfather just the way she had promised she
would do.

"Dear Grandfather. School is wonderful. I'm making a
lot of new friends." She stopped. Heidi knew that wasn't
the absolute truth. But she thought it would be better to
be optimistic about her new home than to worry Grandfather.

In the library, Mrs. Hillary was leading a discussion on
the current situation in Europe. A large map set on an
easel showed the countries involved in the hostilities.
Heidi was trying to concentrate but kept looking out the
window.

"What country is currently trying to expand her borders?" Mrs. Hillary asked the group.

"Germany," Ursula blurted out, pointing to the map.

"Well done, Ursula. What country moved by nation-
alistic fervor to readjust her borders has recently entered
what people are now calling the Great War on the side
of Britain, France, and Russia?"

"Italy," said Ilsa, beating Ursula to the answer.

Mrs. Hillary continued, "And who owns the provinces
she wants?"

"The Austro-Hungarian Empire," answered Gudron.

"Yes, Gudron. The Austro-Hungarian Empire, Germany's friend. But in these turbulent times, who is wise enough to remain neutral?" Mrs Hillary saw Heidi staring out the window. "Switzerland. Heidi, can you show us where Switzerland is."

At the mention of her home, Heidi sat up straight and thought about the question. She walked over to the window instead of to the map and pointed at the distant mountains.

"There," Heidi said softly.

The room erupted with laughter. Mrs. Hillary clapped her hands to restore order to her class. Heidi walked back to her chair feeling crushed by their ridicule. "Switzerland is not a place on a map," Heidi thought, "it is my home."

Mrs. Hillary decided to come to Heidi's rescue. "Girls, let me remind you that Switzerland has the world's oldest democracy, almost seven hundred years. And what is a democracy?" She looked around the room. Ursula tentatively raised her hand. "Yes, Ursula."

"Where the people vote to elect a government?" Ursula said.

"Very good. Yes, where the people have the right, you might even say the responsibility, to elect a government of their choice. Not Germany with its Kaiser or Austria with Emperor Franz Joseph, or even Czar Nicholas of Russia: these are monarchies where the people have no say in their government." Mrs. Hillary saw that Heidi had a question. "Heidi."

"But Britain has a king, doesn't it?" Heidi said. Ursula smothered a giggle.

34

"Yes, it does, but there is a difference. Britain also has a parliament comprised of duly elected representatives of the people, who really govern the country, not the king. Democracy expresses the will of the people and it comes in all sizes and shapes. And I will remind you, it started right over that mountain in Switzerland, almost seven hundred years ago."

The girls filed out of the library still giggling at Heidi. Ilsa caught up to Heidi looking at one of the marble statues in the lobby. Apollo stared back at the girls from his pedestal.

"He's beautiful," Heidi said.

"Someday . . . ," Ilsa said wistfully.

At this moment, Ursula passed them. "You two are positively disgusting," she said without stopping. Ilsa looked back at Ursula and gave her a loud "raspberry." Heidi giggled and walked upstairs with Ilsa.

The bathroom was on the second floor, at the end of the main hallway. Every Friday night, the girls were to take baths after dinner. The large bathroom contained eight large iron-cast bathtubs, each with two faucets of running hot and cold water, a luxury in 1915.

With their towels in hand and dressed in their camisole shifts, the girls lined up, waiting for the next available tub. Heidi was next in line but was puzzled that the girls were bathing in their shifts. This was nothing like the big oak tub at home on the Alm, where she took a bath every Sunday morning. Grandfather would heat the water on the stove inside and pour it over Heidi in the cold morning air.

Heidi didn't think much more about it as she unbuttoned her shift and let it drop to the tiled floor. She stepped into the tub and began to wash. Ilsa took one look at Heidi and was speechless. Suddenly, there was a scream from across the room.

"My God, she's naked!" Ursula shouted.

Heidi covered herself up in embarrassment. "I'm only taking a bath."

"Naked! We're not animals here."

Ilsa defended Heidi. "She's not doing it to annoy you, Ursula."

"You little tramps, you're both revolting!" Ursula retorted, still furious.

Ilsa had had enough. When Ursula turned to leave, Ilsa tossed a large washcloth at her. The sopping wet cloth smacked Ursula in the back of the head. Ilsa smiled as Ursula whirled to catch the culprit. "Who did that? I want to know which one of you perverted little monsters did that. Tell me!" Ursula demanded.

"Ursula, I'm going to tear every hair out of that nasty little head of yours and stuff them down your big fat mouth if you don't leave *now*," Ilsa screamed back.

Silence fell on the room when Mrs. Hillary appeared in the doorway. She was not pleased. "Ilsa, Ursula, go to your room. Heidi, put your clothes on." Heidi dried herself off and put her shift back on.

"Heidi, you may be accustomed to a more rustic experience, and without arguing the merits of naked bathing, suffice it to say we remain clothed here at Brookings. I think we need to have a talk."

"Yes, ma'am." Heidi replied quietly.

Mrs. Hillary stood behind her immaculate Victorian

desk, the prized possession she had brought with her from England. Bundled up in a robe, with her hair still wet, Heidi sat in a high-backed chair directly in front of the long desk. The child seemed so small, so out-of-place, thought Mrs. Hillary. Her heart went out to her new student and she knew she must do something to help.

"Heidi, I know it's been difficult for you here. Yet, your grandfather has given you this wonderful opportunity and we need to make the most of it. Don't you think so?" Heidi slowly nodded her head. "Well, how shall we solve this problem?"

"I'm trying, but it's hard. The other girls are so different."

"I realize that Brookings is an entirely different world for you, Heidi, and I know you've been trying. I really do." Mrs. Hillary moved from behind her desk to the fireplace. On the mantel were old photographs and mementos.

"It wasn't too long ago that I was a stranger here just like you. When I first came to Italy some years ago, I found everything quite different as well. New customs, new people, a new language. At times I felt like giving up. But I came to look upon it all as an adventure. And you must too. New places and new people should be exciting, Heidi."

"Mrs. Hillary, I miss the Alm and Grandfather. And I miss Peter," Heidi blurted out, trying to hold back her tears.

Mrs. Hillary knew she had made a connection. "Who is Peter?"

"He's my best friend and I miss him terribly. He's joined the army and I don't know what will happen to him."

"I see. Well, I'm sure that if your friend Peter can join the army, he's old enough to take care of himself. But you shouldn't worry dear, at least you know he won't have to be in this awful war. Now, Heidi, I think I know how to solve at least one of our problems," Mrs. Hillary said. She walked across the room and opened the door to a large, walk-in closet.

"In here are some extra school clothes left behind by a few of the girls. Now, come here and let's find some things you need." Heidi's eyes popped as she saw stacks of sweaters, bloomers, skirts and shoes.

"How about this blue jumper? This was little Christine's. Such a trouble maker, but really a dear."

"Mrs. Hillary, it's beautiful! Can I really have it?"

"Well, it's not doing anyone any good sitting in this closet. Now, what else can we find for you?"

The two rummaged happily through the closet for the rest of the evening. Heidi knew that she had found a new friend. Later that night, Heidi fell asleep, looking forward for the first time to a new day at Brookings.

case and looked out the car window. They were on the outskirts of Tirano, but already the news of Austria's new offensive, launched only miles away, was having its effect. The captain was witnessing the beginning of the evacuation of Tirano. The sound of the Austrian heavy artillery could be heard in the distance.

Mrs. Hillary studied the Milano newspaper with concern. The headline stated that four Austrian divisions under Count von Smarnersoff had broken through the Italian defense perimeter near Lake Garda the day before yesterday, but twelve Italian divisions had been rushed to the scene and were counterattacking. Being only too familiar with Italian newspapers, Mrs. Hillary knew the situation was probably far worse than had been reported. She got up from her desk and walked to the large window in her study that overlooked the front lawn and gardens where her students were taking their morning exercises. Because of the cold, the girls were all wearing heavy sweaters over their exercise bloomers. Mrs. Hillary made a mental note to have Miss Perry, the new physical education teacher she had engaged from London at the beginning of term, move the morning exercises indoors. Of course, Miss Perry should have thought of that herself, mused Mrs. Hillary, but that was what you had to expect in these times: poor help and few students.

She reflected on past years when the school she had worked so hard to have recognized as a leading girls' school had been full, even with a waiting list. Mrs. Hillary had spent her early childhood in France with her mother and was later sent to join her father in England for her formal education. She had married quite young, but well. George Martin Hillary, some thirty years her senior, was a wealthy man, and when he passed on some ten years after their marriage, Jane Hillary found herself with a good deal of money. Since there had been no children, Jane had no ties in England and soon made her home on Lake Como, in a small villa overlooking the beautiful lake. However, after three rather boring years, Jane was offered Brookings by two ancient English maiden sisters who were anxious to spend their last days in Kent. That had occurred fifteen years ago, and although Jane had poured most of her money into the school, as she had to have everything just so, she had no regrets. She had her girls, and that was the most important thing.

Mrs. Hillary's thoughts returned to her remaining girls exercising on the front lawn. Mrs. Hillary singled out Heidi, who was doing her very best to follow Miss Perry's instructions. "Such a willing child," thought Mrs. Hillary. "She really has adapted quite well in the time we've had her, despite her background. I'll have to get a letter off to her grandfather in the next day or two." Mrs. Hillary was about to return to her desk when she spotted the army car approaching the front entrance.

Heidi and the rest of the girls watched the car pull up by the stone stairs. A tall Italian officer got out of the car and tipped his hat to the girls. Miss Perry didn't quite know what to do, so she blew her whistle. "Young ladies, that will be all for today. Use the side entrance, and I want to see all of you properly changed in the dining room

41

in precisely thirty minutes. . . . Now off with you!" As Ursula led her classmates toward the side entrance on the south side of the mansion, she managed to get a good look at Captain Ornesco as she passed. She was not alone. All the girls gave the distinguished-looking captain at least a glance as they passed by. Mrs. Hillary was at the front doors to greet the captain, who bowed gracefully.

"My apologies, Signora, for disturbing the class. I am Captain Ornesco and I have been instructed to ask for the proprietor, Mrs. Hillary."

"I am Mrs. Hillary, Captain. What may I do for you?"

The captain cleared his throat. He certainly was not enjoying this assignment. "Is there someplace where we can talk? I am here at the request of General Ravenna and it concerns your school."

Mrs. Hillary studied the young captain for only a moment, and then turned and entered the mansion. "Please follow me."

After Captain Ornesco had finished delivering his orders, Mrs. Hillary stood speechless. They were in her study with the door closed. She tried to speak, but no words would come out. Concerned, the captain moved toward her. "Signora, . . . is there something I can get you? Some water perhaps?"

Mrs. Hillary closed her eyes for a moment and then took a deep breath to regain control. "But Captain . . . ?" Mrs. Hillary vainly tried to remember his name.

"Ornesco . . . Roberto, Signora."

"Yes, yes, Captain Ornesco. I know you and the general mean well, and of course who wouldn't want Brookings for their headquarters, but you see, this is a school for young ladies and we still have three weeks to the Christmas break. An idea, Captain. You go back and tell your general that I will definitely consider renting Brookings—and at a reasonable figure I assure you—for the entire four weeks of the Christmas break."

Captain Ornesco, a valiant officer with a distinguished combat record on the eastern front, carefully weighed his options. He knew that the woman before him had heard every word of his orders but, for whatever reason, had either chosen to ignore them altogether or had somehow misunderstood. He could either restate his orders in the most precise terms, or actively take over the school as of this moment, claiming that he had met resistance to his orders, or he could simply leave and let the general handle it. Knowing full well that the latter would most likely get him court-martialed, the captain decided to try once again.

"Signora, I do not think you fully understand. . . ." He looked at his watch. "In precisely two hours the first soldiers from my division will be here at Brookings. By tomorrow at this time there will be over four thousand men bivouacked on your grounds, and on the following day you and the young ladies will have to be gone. That document on your desk is from the Governor of Tirano, ordering you to evacuate Brookings. I am terribly sorry, Mrs. Hillary, but we are at war, and right now the Austrians are not very far away."

Mrs. Hillary's lower lip trembled as she caught the full impact of what the captain was saying. The girls were going to have to leave Brookings. . . . More important, she was going to have to leave. After spending fifteen years and most of her money there, she was being kicked out of her own school and home, and there was absolutely nothing she could do about it short of telling the Austrians to please go back to Austria.

The next morning Mrs. Hillary looked out her bedroom window from the third floor and saw that what the young captain had predicted had indeed come true. The front lawn was covered with soldiers, horses, carts, a few trucks, artillery pieces, and worst of all, the heavy guns were being positioned in her prize rose beds. She might faint, she thought, but no, she must be strong, for today was the day she must say good-bye to her girls. They had all been so brave when she had told them the news. Mrs. Hillary checked herself before her full-length mirror, drew herself up to her full height of five-foot-six, took another deep breath. . . . She reflected that she had been taking a good many deep breaths of late and marched from the room.

The second-floor open hall which was usually used by Mrs. Hillary for assemblies was filled with the twenty girls and the four teachers including Miss Penny who would be leaving. All the girls were dressed in their Brookings uniforms and beside them were suitcases of various sizes and shapes. They stood waiting for their beloved Mrs. Hillary. Heidi, Ursula, Ilsa, and Gudron were with Captain Ornesco off to one side of the hallway and did not have any suitcases. As Mrs. Hillary approached, the room suddenly became very quiet. Jane Hillary faced her girls and took another one of her deep breaths.

"I fear Christmas vacation has arrived a few weeks early this year. Perhaps we'll meet again in the new year. More likely, we will not. If the rest of Europe is any model, the unpleasantness between this country and its neighbors to the north will not be resolved without continued bloodshed. Enough have died already, but unfortunately that is what wars are all about." Mrs. Hillary studied the faces before her.

"I cannot promise you there will be a 'next term' at Brookings, but I'm not going to say good-bye, either, because I am sure we will all be back together when this madness if over. Remember, you may leave Brookings, but Brookings will never leave you. God bless you all."

Mrs. Hillary stood by the large front doors with her arm around Heidi as she, Ursula, Ilsa, and Gudron watched the large army truck filled with the school evacuees as it made its way down the winding driveway. There were tears in Mrs. Hillary's eyes and she held Heidi tightly to her. As the truck was about to disappear around the last bend, the girls on the truck waved for the last time. All Mrs. Hillary could do was raise her hand.

Later that evening Mrs. Hillary was in her study with Heidi and Ilsa and Ursula, who were helping her pack her precious books. Mrs. Hillary tenderly placed the last volume of her rare Shakespeare collection into the packing case and carefully closed the lid. Heidi watched her from the other side of the room, aware of the pain her headmistress was suffering now that she had accepted the fact that she was going to have to leave Brookings. Mrs. Hillary looked around the room, then at the girls, realizing that their task was completed. All the books were now resting in their respective boxes.

"Well, that's over with. Now, let's talk about tomorrow and what we have to do, shall we?" The three girls moved closer. Mrs. Hillary picked up the Tirano train schedule from her desk. "The train for Zurich departs, or I should say is supposed to depart, at eight-ten in the morning, which means we must leave here by no later than seven." Heidi raised her hand.

"Yes, Heidi?"

"What time does the train get to Sils Maria?" Heidi asked. Mrs. Hillary consulted the schedule.

"Four-thirty in the afternoon . . . and Zurich just past midnight. . . . That will mean Ursula, you, Ilsa, and Gudron will stay with me at my hotel, and I will put you all on your respective trains the next morning. Now, I want you girls to finish packing tonight and to be in bed early. I will be up to help you shortly."

The girls followed Ursula out of the room, leaving Mrs. Hillary at her desk. Heidi started to close the study door, but seeing Mrs. Hillary alone and dejected at her desk prompted her to speak out.

"I'm sure we'll all be back very soon, Mrs. Hillary."

Mrs. Hillary couldn't help but smile. Here she was feeling sorry for herself, having to leave her home and school, when Heidi, who had only been at the school for a few months, was trying to console her.

"Thank you, Heidi, but we must face reality, mustn't we? . . . That's all part of growing up, dear."

Heidi looked at her for a moment. There was more she

wanted to say. "Grandfather used to say that sometimes reality or what appears to be real isn't necessarily always the truth, and that there is always hope. Good night, Mrs. Hillary."

Heidi closed the door after her while Mrs. Hillary pondered what she had said. "Can I dare hope? . . . I wonder, but maybe her grandfather's right. What a dreadful place this would be without it."

As Mrs. Hillary moved down the third-floor hallway toward the dormitory, she could hear the screams and laughter of the girls. As she approached the dormitory door it flew open, and Ilsa ran right into Mrs. Hillary's arms just as a feather pillow hit the headmistress squarely in the face. Ursula, clad like Ilsa in a night dress, appeared in the doorway, and upon seeing Mrs. Hillary with feathers all over her, she screamed and ran back into the dormitory.

"Girls!" Mrs. Hillary shouted. Grabbing Ilsa by the arm, she dragged her into the dormitory, which was literally covered in feathers. Another pillow sailed dangerously close to Mrs. Hillary's head. Heidi doubled over with laughter until Gudron slammed her with another pillow. At the same moment Ursula threw a pillow from across the room, and Heidi caught it and brought it down on Gudron's head. There was no stopping the girls; they were simply letting off steam and Mrs. Hillary knew it. She promptly picked up a pillow from a nearby bed and cast it directly at an unsuspecting Ilsa. Seeing that Mrs. Hillary had joined their pillow fight brought screams of delight from the girls, who continued their battle with renewed energy. Pillows and feathers flew in every direction.

Upon entering the mansion, the major directed his men to secure the building while he went in search of Mrs. Hillary. He was determined to have her and the remaining girls out of the house within the hour. The major first checked Mrs. Hillary's study, but finding no one there, he started up the main stairway. On reaching the second floor hallway, he paused to catch his breath. The major was overweight, and although he often thought of dieting he couldn't give up the rich food that he desperately craved. Believing he heard voices coming from the next floor, the major cocked his head and listened carefully. Yes, there they were again. "Signora Hillary!" he called out, but there was no reply. Having no choice but to investigate, the major slowly started up the stairs to the third floor.

The Brookings Pillow War of 1915 was over; Mrs. Hillary, having sought a negotiated peace whose terms had been rejected, had finally no other option but to raise the white and torn pillowcase signifying unconditional surrender. The victors surveyed the battleground and marveled at the mess. Feathers were everywhere, on the floor, still floating in the air, in the girls' and Mrs. Hillary's hair. Mrs. Hillary sat on one of the beds, attempting to catch her breath. She was the first to see the apparition moving toward them through the sea of feathers. It stopped a few feet from her and, in utter amazement at the destruction, finally spoke:

"Signora Hillary. This . . . this will not do. My soldiers were to sleep here tonight. You and your girls are saboteurs, and I am reporting this to the governor." The major would have gone on, but a floating feather lodged itself in his mouth.

Mrs. Hillary slowly got up from the bed and brushed herself off, then eyed the fat Italian officer. "And you are?" Mrs. Hillary asked.

"Major Rieti, the governor's military aide," he said, spitting out the offending feather.

"May I remind you, Major, that you are first of all in my house . . . at least until tomorrow at eleven, at which time you can be assured that I and my four remaining young ladies will have departed. Now, if you would be good enough to remove yourself from these premises, I will reconsider filing a formal complaint with your governor and the British ambassador." The major tried to speak, but no words would come out. "As for your ridiculous charge of sabotage, these are my linens, my pillows, and my feathers! Good night, Major!"

Waving away more feathers, the major stood up straight, which left him somewhat shorter than Mrs. Hillary. "It is you, Signora, and your girls who are to leave, by order of the governor, tonight, not tomorrow!"

"Impossible, Major. Are you going to take the responsibility of throwing these girls out into the night with nowhere to go, and creating an international incident, which I assure you it will?"

Weighing this for a moment, the major suddenly smiled, knowing he now had the solution. "Ah, Signora, no one wants an incident, and I must apologize for my clumsy manners, but the Austrians are very close . . . very close, and as you say, we are responsible. I will immediately make arrangements for the young ladies and yourself on behalf of my governor. Speed and safety are everything, and if you would please see that everyone is dressed and downstairs in half an hour, it would be most expeditious. Fighting may break out at any time, Signora."

Mrs. Hillary was suspicious, but if the rotund major could provide adequate housing for all of them tonight and get them away from the fighting, it might be best. As always, Mrs. Hillary thought of her girls first. "Very well, Major, in half an hour, then."

The major attempted a bow, but his large stomach got in the way, so he saluted instead, which brought a giggle from Heidi. Scowling, the major turned and made his way back toward the dormitory entrance through a cloud of feathers.

Gudron looked up at Mrs. Hillary and said, "What a fatty!"

With Mrs. Hillary in the lead, umbrella in hand, followed by Ursula, then Heidi, Ilsa, and finally Gudron, all wearing their uniforms and with heads held high, the Brookings ladies proceeded down the stairs of the main hallway. A smiling Major Rieti greeted them in the center of the hallway. He was flanked on each side by his soldiers. Mrs. Hillary stopped in front of the major.

"Very well, Major, we are here. May I inquire as to our lodgings?"

The major gave her an even wider smile and snapped his fingers. From the study door, dressed in his black cape and hat, Signor Bonelli slithered to the major's side. In true snakelike fashion, Bonelli bowed low to Mrs. Hillary, who reacted by drawing back in horror, gathering her girls to her side. Quickly perceiving what was happening, she turned in anger to the major. But before she could speak he withdrew a document from his tunic.

"Signora Hillary, these are difficult times, as you know. The governor, realizing that the safety of your young ladies is absolutely essential, called upon his old friend Signor Bonelli for help. Signor Bonelli has graciously offered to accept your girls at Saint Mary's for the duration of the Austrians' siege of Tirano."

"This is preposterous! We have no intention of spending one second in this degenerate's diseased orphanage!" Mrs. Hillary snapped.

"Signor Bonelli's invitation does not, unfortunately, include you, Signora. The governor, in his wisdom, however, has made arrangements for you to stay briefly at a small hotel nearby." The major signaled to his men, who moved in to take the girls. One of the soldiers attempted to separate Ursula from Mrs. Hillary but was given a resounding clout on the head by Mrs. Hillary's umbrella.

"Take that, you pervert!" She swung the umbrella in a wide arc and another soldier fell while Signor Bonelli and the major made a strategic withdrawal to the other side of the hallway.

"Stop her," screamed the Major.

However, Mrs. Hillary defended her girls—she would

do so with her life if need be. The umbrella struck again and again as the major's soldiers attempted in vain to grab the weapon. One soldier was able to grab Ilsa from behind but was forced to let her go when Heidi, Ursula, and Gudron began kicking him. Then, suddenly, it was all over, as one burly soldier managed to take the umbrella away from Mrs. Hillary. Two others pinned Mrs. Hillary's arms while the major ordered his men to get the girls outside. Signor Bonelli led the way as the soldiers dragged and carried the four screaming girls out the main door.

The major triumphantly made his way to Mrs. Hillary, who was still being held by two soldiers. As she watched the fat, gloating major's approach, Mrs. Hillary was able to pull one arm free to wipe her tears away. The major motioned that the soldier who was still holding Mrs. Hillary's other arm should let her go.

"Once you have regained your control, Signora, one of my men will escort you to your hotel. You will be quartered there until the governor deems it safe for you to continue your journey."

"I take it, then, that I am your prisoner?" Mrs. Hillary asked.

The major smiled. "Not at all, Signora. It is only for your protection. . . . Remember, the Austrians?"

"Oh, yes, the Austrians. Major Rieti, I promise you one thing. When this is over, you are going to rue the day this ever happened. And Major, I will give you one bit of advice." Mrs. Hillary moved closer to the major and looked directly into his puffy eyes. "I would make very sure if I were you that those children are well looked after at that awful orphanage."

Mustering every ounce of dignity at her command and without even a backward glance at the major, Mrs. Hillary, flanked by her two escorts, walked proudly out the front door.

CHAPTER 5

The black carriage thundered through the wet, cobble-stone streets of Tirano. Bonelli drove the horses himself as if the devil were snapping at their heels. The children from Brookings were now his. He had lived long enough in the shadow of The Brookings Academy for Girls and Mrs. Jane Hillary. These four new children would add to his collection of nearly ninety. If Bonelli had his way, Brookings would never reopen. "Signora Bonelli will be happy tonight," he thought.

Inside the carriage, Heidi clung to a railing with all her might. Hard wooden benches along the sides were the only seats. The girls were tossed from one side to the other. The carriage lurched violently to the left as it took a corner at high speed, throwing Gudron toward the back. Heidi grabbed her by the waist before she could hurt herself. The girls were terrrified. Where were they going?

Ursula and Ilsa were by the door, holding on to the bars on the small windows. In the streets, people were loading furniture onto horse-drawn carts. As the rain poured down, families were leaving their homes, traveling south, away from the Austro-Hungarian border just fifteen miles to the north. The girls had been taken from their home and did not know what the future held for them at St. Mary's.

A servant opened the gates when he heard the horses and carriage approaching. An ominous moan came from the old hinges on the gates as they opened to reveal St. Mary's, a converted factory on the edge of town. Bonelli drove through the gates and around to the back of the building. At the loading docks he pulled the horses to a stop. He kept the whip in his hand when he opened the door of the carriage to find four frightened faces staring back at him.

"Get out!" were the first orders he barked.

The girls were herded into a large, dark room. At the end of a long table there was a single, flickering lantern. Heidi saw a shadow move in the corner.

"The dark can be so comforting," said the shadow. A hollow whistling came down the cold fireplace. "New arrivals?"

"Yes. From the Brookings School, no less. Four . . . young . . . girls. . . ." Bonelli said, taking his time with each word as he spoke to the person moving in the shadows. The lantern lit the face of Signora Bonelli as she moved to the table.

Heidi found the signora's piercing eyes staring directly at her. Signora Bonelli's dark hair was pulled tightly back in a bun, leaving her entire ash-white face for all to see. She moved closer to the girls. Ilsa let out a sneeze in the damp room.

"Poor little things, you must be so cold. And hungry." The Signora held Ilsa's chin firmly and moved her face close. "Your Brookings days are over, little thing. You all must face what lies ahead in this world. Changes can be sudden, can't they." The Signora allowed herself a tiny laugh that sent a shiver down Heidi's back.

They were taken to a room upstairs. Heidi could barely see the flat, hard beds that were lined up against the wall, nor the sleeping children covered only in tattered blankets. From the corner came a squealing sound that Heidi refused to think about. Ursula jumped as something brushed across her feet.

"Not a word from you! Do you think you'll get any sympathy from me because you're not in your cozy beds at Brookings? Not from me or anyone else here." The Signora never raised her voice but instead lowered it in a menacing whisper when she wanted to be heard.

Heidi, Ilsa, Gudron, and Ursula were each assigned a bunk with one thin blanket. "Girls are on this side and that is the boys' side. There will be no talking. I am down the hall with the Signor." Signora Bonelli walked to the door and turned to the girls. With a sharp breath, the lantern light was extinguished, enshrouding the room in darkness. "We will be listening."

———

A rat nibbled on a piece of stolen bread under the table where the thin legs of small children dangled as they ate the measly breakfast put out for them. Hard pieces of bread and a rancid-smelling broth were on each plate in small portions. It was after dawn when the orphans and the four new arrivals were assembled for a meal—if it could be called that.

Ursula looked around the room they had been taken to the night before. The dining area took up only one part of the room. Large wooden vats of soap boiled at the far end; suspended above them were a series of troughs channeling the fats and lye into the vats. Running down the center of the room into a large drainage grate was a steady stream of viscous, soapy scum. The stench of sweat blended with the sickly-sweet scent of perfume that was added to the soap mixture, making it even more difficult to eat breakfast.

"Someone must speak to him, Ursula," Heidi said as she poked her piece of crusted bread. The four girls sat together at the far end of the table. The Bonellis were enjoying full breakfast at the head of the table while the orphans ate in silence.

"No. Mrs. Hillary will be here soon. We'll wait for her," Ursula said, afraid to confront the Bonellis.

Heidi looked at her bowl of smelly broth and then at the orphans with their pinched faces and hollow eyes. She recognized the little girl she had met at the Tirano train station. Clarissa had her eyes on her plate, for this food was all she would get until nightfall. The little girl noticed a large cockroach headed for her plate and smashed her hand down on the bug. No food could be spared. Heidi left her seat and started to walk to the head of the table. All eyes looked up as Heidi made her way toward the Bonellis.

Giovanni could not resist smiling as he watched the nice girl from the train station approach the nasty Bonellis. No one ever got up from the table before Signora Bonelli had finished her meal. He wanted to tell Heidi that she was heading for trouble.

Signora Bonelli looked up from her omelet to find Heidi gazing hungrily at the eggs and gooey cheese on her plate. "I did not give you permission to leave your seat. I might confiscate your breakfast for that."

Heidi addressed Signor Bonelli, which did not please the Signora. "Ilsa, Gudron, and Ursula and I would like to leave now. Thank you for giving us a place to stay for the night, but we really must go now." Heidi thought it was best to be polite but firm. Her words echoed through the large room, giving the rest of the orphans the chance to hear what was going on at the head of the table.

Bonelli gave the girl in front of him a quick glance and finished his omelet. He laid his knife and fork down at precisely the correct angle and wiped his thin lips with the corner of his cloth napkin.

"I do appreciate good manners as you can see. Interrupting the headmaster's breakfast is bad manners. You must watch that. Now, as for your request. I am sorry but this is not possible." Bonelli gave his wife a look, which the Signora returned with a nod for him to continue.

"I have already contacted your parents and assured

them of your safety. I told them it was impossible to guarantee your safety if you traveled home under the present hostilities. They gratefully requested I keep you here with me. So, there is no cause for alarm. Now take your seat."

Heidi didn't move an inch. "I don't believe you."

This time Signora Bonelli answered. "Watch your tongue! Your first lesson here is that impudence will be punished. For all her pompous, upper-class airs, your Mrs. Hillary doesn't seem to know how to teach young girls to behave. But I do. For that outburst, you lose your breakfast."

"And her dinner," Bonelli added, trying to hold some line of authority over his wife. He gave Heidi a shove with his bony finger. Heidi was quite shaken. She knew Grandfather would not have given anyone permission to keep her locked up in some orphanage. Giovanni gave Heidi a big smile when their eyes met. He thought she was a brave girl.

Heidi sat back down next to Ursula. Even Ursula had to admire what Heidi had done. Heidi looked frightened and said, "I think we've been stolen."

That morning the four girls learned what the Bonellis had is store for them at St. Mary's. They were put to work in the soap factory with the other orphans. Under the watchful eye of Signora Bonelli, Ilsa and Gudron carried buckets of hot soap from the vats to the molding room. There they poured the thick, steaming soap over a large wooden board that had bar-shaped molds carved in its surface. When the soap had cooled, the board would be turned over and out would come the individual bars, which were then wrapped in pretty tissue paper with the label "From Saint Mary's Orphanage."

As the Signora watched Ilsa and Gudron, they spilled some soap on the floor. She quickly reprimanded them: "There will be no waste, you sloppy little children."

"Gudron has some soap in her eye," Ilsa said as she tended Gudron, who was squinting and rubbing her eye.

The Signora brushed her hand on the molding board, picking up some soap, and rubbed her finger in Gudron's other eye. "Now she has soap in both her eyes. Now, back to work."

Heidi and Giovanni were assigned to swing the trough suspended from the ceiling from the full vat to the empty one. The whale fat and lye would roll down the trough and plop into the vat. The vats were heated by gas burners, which Giovanni had to light every morning. Giovanni told Heidi she would eventually get used to the sting of the soap.

"There isn't going to be time for that," Heidi told him with great determination.

"Careful, Bonelli is watching us from the balcony up there. He's very smart at business. The governor pays him money for each child here. He gets paid to keep us, and then he has slaves for his factory." Giovanni motioned to Heidi that it was time to swing the big trough to the other vat. Once Bonelli saw that the trough was in place he pulled a lever, releasing the soap mixture and sending it splattering into the vat.

Giovanni continued, "A lot of the children here aren't even orphans. Some are runaways he caught. Others are just lost. Once he gets his hooks into you, he never lets go."

"Why doesn't anyone run away?" Heidi asked. Giovanni didn't answer but simply gave Heidi a sad smile. They would if they could.

Above the children, on the balcony, the Bonellis looked down on their workers. Bonelli pointed to Heidi. "She is a good worker, that one. She's strong."

"That's what you said about the Hungarian girl and she died. One of these days your greed with be the end of you," his wife warned him in a condescending tone. Bonelli ignored her and walked down the steps to check the loading dock.

He walked past Ursula, who was carrying a box of finished soaps to the loading dock. Bonelli stopped to brush his hand over Ursula's fine brown hair. She was so young and pretty. Ursula ducked and continued struggling with the heavy load. Bonelli laughed and walked out. Heidi saw that Ursula was alone and quietly walked over to her. She took one side of the box to help Ursula.

"Why hasn't Mrs. Hillary come?" Heidi whispered, knowing Signora Bonelli was probably close by.

"She will. Soon," said Ursula, trying to sound optimistic.

"What if she doesn't? What if she can't?"

"She will. She must!"

"Ursula, let's get Ilsa and Gudron and run away."

"Don't be silly, we'd never make it. We can't even get to Ilsa and Gudron; they're keeping us separated. The only sensible thing to do is wait for Mrs. Hillary."

Heidi put her end of the box down and pulled Ursula

off to the side. "Listen to me. What if she doesn't come?" Heidi spoke slowly to make sure Ursula understood what she was trying to say.

Ursula lost her temper. "Look! She wouldn't just abandon us. Maybe you, but not me and the others. You don't know her. I do and she'll be here."

Heidi began to shout. "What if she's ill and she can't come! What if my grandfather's ill; what if he's dying? Why didn't he send for me?" Signora Bonelli was suddenly upon them.

"What do you think you're doing?"

Heidi began to cry and shouted with all her might, "I don't belong here. I'm not an orphan. I have a grandfather!"

CHAPTER 6

One bright afternoon, Peter climbed the path to Grandfather's hut on the Alm. He had been in Sils Maria for basic training with the rest of the Swiss Army volunteers from the southern region of Switzerland. They trained five days a week but had the weekends to themselves. Peter normally stayed in Sils Maria on his days off, making new friends and studying military manuals. He and his fellow trainees knew they would probably never see the war move into Switzerland, but war brought no guarantees. He felt older in his dark blue uniform with its gold buttons down the front. There were no stripes of rank or authority yet, but they would come in time.

This weekend he had returned to Dörfli to see his family and to find out whether Grandfather had any news of Heidi. Peter, along with the rest of the world, had learned of Austria's daring push across the Dolomite Mountains into Italy. If northern Italy was to become a battleground, he knew Heidi would most likely be on her way home. He had stopped by the village post office, which occupied a small corner of the general store, and found a telegram from Tirano for Grandfather, which he decided to deliver personally.

Peter knocked on the door of the large wooden hut and entered to find Grandfather finishing his lunch of goat cheese and bread. In the large hearth, a fire was busy warming the entire hut. The afternoon mountain air gave Peter a chill on his long walk up the Alm and he moved immediately to the fireplace.

"It is good to see you. I have a telegram from Tirano for you. It was at the store waiting for you but I thought it looked important and I brought it straight away," Peter said in a rush. He had always been a little intimidated by Grandfather, a man of few words and fewer compliments.

"You left your post to visit Dörfli?" Grandfather inquired as he took the telegram from Peter's hand.

"No, we are free to leave on Saturdays and Sundays," Peter explained, standing very straight by the fireplace. "I usually stay in Sils Maria in the barracks. To study."

Grandfather knew Peter was looking for a kind word about his new station in life as a soldier. "That's a fine uniform for such a young man."

"Thank you, sir," Peter said, not certain how to take the remark. "Of course, I'm not the youngest in the troop. Some are only sixteen. The army is accepting volunteers under twenty because of the war. I guess it's natural for children to think they can be soldiers. I try to look out for them." Peter deepened his voice to convey some sense of authority.

"I see. I guess a man of seventeen does command the respect of children."

"Eighteen, actually," Peter gently corrected Grandfather.

Grandfather had tested the young man enough. "Well, the uniform is a nice fit, Peter," he said reassuringly. "Have some lunch."

Grandfather turned away from Peter to read the telegram. He too had heard the news about the Austrian offensive. His first thought was to send for Heidi immediately, but he had decided to wait for word from Heidi or the school, to show confidence in his granddaughter. Two days before, Grandfather had received a telegram from Mrs. Jane Hillary. The Italian Army had taken over the school buildings and ordered the students evacuated from Tirano. Mrs. Hillary was personally going to escort Heidi and three other girls to Switzerland. Grandfather was waiting for word as to their time of arrival in Sils Maria, where he would meet Heidi's train.

Reading the new telegram from Mrs. Hillary, Grandfather knew something was wrong. "Peter! Heidi's been sent to an orphanage in Tirano . . . St. Mary's. How can this be?" Grandfather handed the telegram back to Peter and sat down.

Peter read the last paragraph, ". . . temporarily at St. Mary's orphanage due to the evacuation. Travel to Switzerland delayed until I can collect girls from orphanage.

Do not worry. Regards, Jane Hillary, Headmistress, Brookings Academy for Girls."

Grandfather moved to the door and pulled his coat from the hook on the wall. "I am going to get her myself. An orphanage! My granddaughter is not an orphan. What is that Mrs. Hillary doing? She calls herself 'headmistress.' "

"Grandfather. You can't. The railway has been taken over by the army in Italy. You'd never get through."

"Heidi can't make the journey alone."

"I'll send a cable from my post. I'll make sure it gets through. If we don't hear anything I'll go to Italy and bring her back."

"I have an old man's imagination. There are things I am unable to do." Grandfather sighed and hung his coat back on the wall. "Peter, send the telegram to Mrs. Hillary. We will wait for news. But we will not wait long."

The buckets of raw soap were painfully heavy on Ursula's and Heidi's young arms. Punished for their scene by the loading docks earlier that day, the two girls faced the shuttered windows trembling with the weight of the two buckets they each were forced to hold up at arm's length. One of the Bonellis' factory overseers was watching the two girls. He particularly enjoyed seeing that their eyes were burning from the lye in the buckets.

Ursula whispered, "This is your fault. If you hadn't had a temper tantrum like some baby, my eyes and arms wouldn't . . ." Ursula saw something through the broken shutter. Someone was getting out of an automobile. Yes, it was . . . Mrs. Hillary!

"Heidi, look down there. It's Mrs. Hillary. Thank God!" Heidi let out a gasp when she saw Mrs. Hillary take off her duster and goggles and walk toward the building.

"No talking, ladies," the overseer snapped. He walked over to the girls and ladled some more slop into their buckets, increasing the already unmanageable weight.

Jane Hillary was a determined woman. She had come for the girls and wasn't going to take no for an answer. She stopped on the stoop of the building and looked up. There was an evil-looking woman staring at her from the second-floor window. Mrs. Hillary took a deep breath and walked into St. Mary's Orphanage.

In the lobby, Mrs. Hillary was appalled at what she saw. Dirty-faced, emaciated children in torn and filthy clothes marched past her through a door. She looked in vain for the girls and thought, "This is how my girls are being cared for."

Signora Bonelli took Mrs. Hillary upstairs to the office, away from any view of the factory or the children. Wanting to show Mrs. Hillary every courtesy, the Signora offered her coffee.

"No, Signora. What I want is the four girls who were taken from Brookings by force."

Bonelli sat behind his desk trying to look like the headmaster of a school. He had pictures of children playing football and various trophies that he had bought at a flea market in Milano. "Mrs. Hillary, they were escorted to St. Mary's by order of the governor, who was in turn under orders from the military to vacate Brookings for use as divisional headquarters. These things happen during wartime. The children will be released only to their parents when they arrive. If they arrive."

"The children's parents have been notified that I will be escorting them home. How can their parents travel with the railway taken over by the army and the war getting closer every day? No sir, I am not going to allow my girls—for whom I have responsibility, not the governor—to stay in this decrepit, disgusting, filthy institution that is not healthy for even the rats that live here. In great numbers, may I add." Mrs. Hillary finished her tirade hoping to convince the Bonellis of her resolve.

Signora Bonelli was truly insulted, but she was not going to let her temper get the better of her. "Forgive us, Mrs. Hillary, if we do not have all the creature comforts of a school as opulent and ostentatious as the late Brookings School. We do what we can with what we have for these unfortunate orphans. If God has seen fit to put these children in our hands, we will do our best to raise them as disciplined, well-mannered, hard-working little citizens. Which is more than one can say for the country club you ran. But that is all in the past, isn't it," the Signora responded, quite pleased with herself.

"Discipline comes from education, Signora, not from forced labor in a sewer. I will have no part in this conversation about Brookings. Now, Signor Bonelli, will you give me my children or will I be forced to go the British consulate?"

Bonelli saw that diplomacy was not going to work here and his wife was not helping the situation. "First, the four girls are not *your* children, but they *were* your students.

Second, Mrs. Hillary, the British consulate has no jurisdiction here in Tirano. Furthermore, your students are not British citizens. As I assume you are, the consulate should spend its time arranging safe passage for you back to London, which would rid us of your selfish efforts."

Mrs. Hillary clenched her umbrella tightly and swallowed the lump that had arisen in her throat. "What an evil, nasty man," she thought. She raised her umbrella and slammed it down on the desk. "I am going to have these four children back in my care one way or the other, Signor Bonelli. I don't know exactly what scheme you have arranged with your governor, but I assure you, St. Mary's has not seen the last of me." With that said, Mrs. Hillary turned and walked quickly out of the office. Signora Bonelli followed behind her to make sure she went directly to her car.

Mrs. Hillary got into her car and sat there for a moment. A column of armored vehicles were parading down the street outside the orphanage. It was hard to think with the noise from the cars and trucks, but she knew Bonelli was right about the British consulate. The girls were not British citizens and the consulate would be reluctant to intercede in a local dispute with its new ally, Italy. She put her goggles on and started the motor. Mrs. Hillary decided she would go directly to the governor. With the noise in the street, she couldn't hear the two girls pounding on the window above and calling her name.

Heidi and Ursula watched Mrs. Hillary's car pull away. Ursula turned from the window heartbroken that Mrs. Hillary hadn't arranged for their release from the orphanage. She missed Mrs. Hillary and Brookings so much.

"Ursula, they won't let us go," Heidi said with a great sadness.

"Well, Mrs. Hillary will be back. She just has to get us out of here."

"We have to try to get out of here ourselves."

"And go where?" asked Ursula despondently.

Heidi looked at Ursula, puzzled by her remark. "Home, Ursula. We could all go home."

Ursula snapped back, "She'll be back. I just know it."

"What do you know, young lady," Bonelli inquired, walking up behind them and giving Ursula and Heidi a fright. They turned to find Bonelli leering at them with great interest.

"I know Mrs. Hillary will be back to get us," Ursula said calmly.

"No she won't. Mrs. Hillary will let your parents come for you. Brookings is closed for good and she no longer has any responsibility for you. You will have to become accustomed to your new home. You must miss all the treats Mrs. Hillary used to give you. Well, we have treats here too." Bonelli took from his pockets a foil-wrapped chocolate. The other orphans turned from their work to stare at the candy.

Bonelli moved very close to Ursula. "Have a chocolate. I know you want one. They are so delicious. This one has a raspberry center. Come on." Bonelli unwrapped the piece of candy and put it in Ursula's hand.

Ursula started to tremble. This man frightened her. She could see the rest of the children looking at her as if they

70

would kill to eat it. She took the chocolate from Bonelli and brought it to her mouth. Looking directly at him, Ursula threw the candy to the ground and crushed it with her shoe.

Bonelli heard several of the children laugh at him. He grabbed Ursula's hair. "You little tramp."

Bonelli gave Ursula a small brush and a bucket of water. "Scrub every inch of this floor," he ordered with such a bite in his voice that she thought he was going to hit her. Heidi stood off to the side, unable to do anything. Signora Bonelli walked into the room carrying of a box of lye.

"If your Mrs. Hillary thinks this place is so filthy and disgusting, then Brookings can clean it up," Signora Bonelli barked. She shoved Heidi to the floor with Ursula. "Both of you will have no dinner or any other meal until this room is spotless." The Signora took a box of soap powder and dumped it in the bucket and shook the remaining powder over Ursula and Heidi. Bonelli kicked the bucket of water over, splashing the girls and covering the cement floor.

A crowd of orphans gathered to watch the girls' punishment. Giovanni was at the back of the group, unable to get a good view of the proceedings. The water from the bucket went streaming between the feet of the orphans and into the drainage grate in the center of the room. With great interest Giovanni watched the water pour through a large round grate and swish down into the sewer. His attention to the drain was broken when Bonelli bellowed at the top of his lungs for everyone to get back to work.

CHAPTER 7

Heidi and Ursula had worked late into the night, with the Bonellis taking turns watching over them. Their hands were bruised and burned from the lye and their knees were scraped bloody from crawling across the floor for hours. Heidi lay in her bed exhausted and frightened of the prospect of even one more day at the hands of the Bonellis. She heard a scuffling sound from a far corner of the room. At first she thought it was a pack of rats, but then saw Giovanni making his way stealthily to her bedside.

Giovanni froze when he heard familiar voices down the hall. The Bonellis were having one of their screaming arguments. When he realized they were not coming toward the dormitory, he ran silently to Heidi's bed and knelt in the shadows between two beds.

"Heidi, are you all right?" Giovanni whispered. "Can you walk?"

"Yes. My knees hurt, but they're okay. Walk where?" Heidi asked.

"Heidi, I found a way to get out of here. But I need your help. It's too heavy to move myself."

"What's too heavy?" Heidi asked excitedly.

"Ssh, keep your voice down. The Bonellis will hear and we'll be stuck here forever." Giovanni moved closer so Heidi could hear his plan. Heidi thought it was the only chance they had to escape.

"I have to get Ilsa and Gudron. And Ursula. Stay here." Heidi went to wake the others. Ilsa and Gudron got dressed while Heidi whispered the plan to Ursula.

"You must be joking. Crawl down there? Disgusting!" Ursula protested.

"What's more disgusting: that or staying here? There's no time to argue. Ursula, we're going with or without you. You can wait here if you want for your parents or Mrs. Hillary. But we won't!"

Ursula thought about that for a moment. "All right, I'll come."

The four girls and Giovanni crept silently past the Bonellis' bedroom, which was now silent. The group joined hands and filed along the darkened hallway and down the stairs to the main room. The only light came from the moonlight seeping through the skylight.

Giovanni and Heidi crouched over the large drainage grate in the center of the floor. They both knew that if anybody came into the room there would be no place to hide. The two of them began to lift the cast-iron grate. It took every ounce of strength they had between them. Expressions of pain filled their faces as the unwieldy grate finally began to loosen from its setting. They rested the grate next to the opening they had just uncovered. Ursula bent over the opening and peered into the murky abyss. A noxious stench arose from the open sewer.

"Pew! Heidi, we can't go down there," she said in a hushed voice.

"It's that or stay here. I'll go first," Heidi whispered back.

"I'll go next," said a little voice behind the group. They turned around to find Clarissa, who had followed them from the dormitory. She was ready for a journey: she had brought a warm sweater, a scarf, and her small teddy bear, which she kept hidden under her bed.

"She's not coming with us. The more people we have, the harder it will be to escape," Ursula counseled.

Heidi didn't think twice. "She's coming. I'll look after her. Now let's go."

Heidi took a deep breath and started down the ladder built into the side of the sewer wall. Each metal rung was covered with the slippery, soapy fluid that drained from the room every day. Heidi's foot slid from under her, but she grabbed tightly with her hands and steadied herself. Carefully, she lowered herself to the bottom of the sewer. Her shoes squished in and sucked up whatever ghastly mess had collected in the tunnel. The vile odor made Heidi gag, but she refused to let the horror of the situation sway her resolve to escape from the prison above her. She waved the rest of the group down. Giovanni helped each of the girls start down the ladder, telling them to hold on tightly and not to look down.

Ursula forced herself to descend the ladder, cursing Heidi's name under her breath every step of the way. When she landed in the fetid muck below, she turned to Heidi. "Now, you better know how to get us out of here!" Bringing up the rear, Giovanni climbed halfway down the ladder and moved the grate back into place above him. He cringed at the scraping sound it made against the cement. The grate stopped an inch from its setting. Giovanni pulled with all his might, but it would not budge. Hoping no one would notice that the grate was ajar, he joined the rest of the group.

Ursula, still mad about Heidi's overriding her decision on letting Clarissa come along, took the little girl's teddy bear and threw it into the watery muck. "If you're coming with us, then grow up. No dolls or teddy bears!" Clarissa saw her little friend lying facedown in the sewer. But she knew Ursula was right; she had to be very brave. Anyway, now she had new friends. Clarissa moved closer to Heidi and took her hand.

Heidi looked down the dark tunnel ahead of them. There was a tiny speck of light in the distance that she prayed came from the street. They all joined hands again and began sloshing through the tunnel. Each step they took echoed through the dark, narrow tunnel.

Ilsa held tightly onto to Giovanni's hand. She didn't mind the darkness as much as the horrific odor. At the end of the line, Gudron pinched her nose with her free hand.

"Gudron, look on the bright side. At least we're not in

the Paris sewers," Ilsa said, trying to comfort her friend.

"How could the Paris sewers be any worse?"

"My uncle says they're filled with giant alligators," Ilsa said confidently.

Gudron's face froze. "What if they travel?" she thought. She clamped her eyes shut and continued to hold her nose.

Heidi and Giovanni led the group down the sewer tunnel, moving slowing through the sludgy mess at their feet. Giovanni did not know what they would find at the other end of the tunnel, but it had to be better than what they had just left. He had only been at St. Mary's a short time, but it was long enough to know he never wanted to be put back in there with the merciless Bonellis. Having lived in the horrible conditions at the orphanage, Giovanni took no notice of the many rats scurrying through the tunnel. Heidi knew the rodents were more afraid of people than the children were of them. But they were all still scared.

They came to a fork in the tunnel and stood in a group to decide which way to turn. To the right, they could see the light coming from another grate several hundred yards ahead. They hoped it came from a streetlamp outside the orphanage. To the left, there was hardly any light shining through the tunnel. Giovanni fished around in his pockets for one of the matches he had stolen from the workroom. He took a wooden match and struck it against the wall. The match caught and sparkled to life, throwing light on what lay ahead. Ursula screamed!

There, against the side of the tunnel, was a small skeleton, a child's skeleton. It was leaning against a wall, still

76

in its tattered clothes. The rest of the girls gasped in horror at the ghoulish sight. Giovanni saw the skeleton and, in his fright, dropped the match in the water. Suddenly it was dark again. Heidi grabbed Clarissa and ran down the tunnel on the right.

"Run!" Heidi screamed. God only knew what else was in there. Racing for the light, no one cared anymore about the rats or the stench; they just wanted to get out. Giovanni dashed up the ladder to the grating above and called to Heidi to help him open the metal covering. Heidi climbed up to Giovanni and hooked one arm over the top rung. Once again, it took all their strengh to move the grate. They pushed the cover up and slid it off to one side. Giovanni and Heidi both peeked over the opening. They saw the cobblestone street at the entrance to St. Mary's. They were free!

One by one they climbed out of the sewer and the horror below. The sun was just about to rise over Tirano. Soon they would be missed and the Bonellis would surely come after them. Their faces and clothes were covered with dirt and grime. Clarissa took her scarf off and wiped her face. Giovanni and Heidi were catching their breath as a milk wagon pulled into the street. Drawn by a single horse, the wagon halted outside the gates of the orphanage. The milkman deposited a crate of milk and eggs at the gate and picked up the empty bottles left the night before. After putting the empties in the back of the truck, the milkman moved the wagon out into the street.

Running after the wagon, Giovanni opened the back door and jumped into the van. He waved frantically to the rest of the group to follow. The girls made a dash for the wagon, which was moving quickly down the street. Ilsa, Gudron, and Ursula grabbed onto the back and pulled themselves in. Heidi was dragging Clarissa along when suddenly Clarissa lost her grip on Heidi's hand and fell on the cobblestones. Heidi dashed back, picked Clarissa up in her arms, and ran after the moving dairy wagon. Clarissa was light enough to boost up to Giovanni, who pulled her in. Heidi climbed in and shut the door. The wagon turned the corner and headed north, leaving St. Mary's in the early morning. The children could not see Paulo, with tears in his eyes, looking down on them from a window above. He wished he was going with them.

Signora Bonelli pulled the little orphan up in front of the breakfast table. There was no food on the table, nor would there be until the Bonellis learned how the children had escaped and where they had gone.

"All of you must be hungry. Poor Paulo is hungry too. But neither Paulo nor you will have anything to eat unless Paulo tells us what happened last night."

"I didn't help them." Paulo's voice was quivering.

"Where did they go? I saw you at the window," Signora Bonelli pressed.

"I don't know. I didn't see them." Paulo answered back.

Bonelli was pacing the floor, trying to figure out how they escaped. All the entrances to the building were locked from the inside with keys that only he and his wife had. The windows were all on the second or third floors and there was no rope or ladder to be found. Then he saw it. In the center of the room, one of the sewer grates was dislodged. They went through the sewer tunnel beneath the building!

"Signora," he shrieked, pointing to the grate.

Signora Bonelli gasped in horror as she looked at the grate. "My God, they've seen." She turned back to little Paulo and pulled his hair sharply. "There is no time to waste. Tell me now or you and all of your little friends will be paying for this incident until you leave St. Mary's, and that is going to be a very long time from now."

Paulo looked at the Signora's fierce eyes. He knew she meant what she said. He turned to the rest of the orphans, who were looking at him with wide, sorrowful eyes. He knew they wanted him to confess, but they weren't going to tell him to. The runaways still had a chance to escape from the Bonellis, but these children would remain. He would not be responsible for punishing the rest of the orphans.

With great guilt in his heart, Paulo moved to the window where he had seen the children and said, "The milkman." He prayed Giovanni and the girls were far enough away. Looking out the window, Paulo whispered, "Forgive me."

Bonelli ran for the door where his horse was waiting. He had to catch the children and bring them back to the orphanage. They would be sorry they ever tried to leave. He mounted his black steed and whipped the horse with his riding crop.

"Ha, the milkman," he cackled as rider and horse raced through the gates of St. Mary's.

———

The children popped their heads out of the van when it clattered to a stop at a farm north of Tirano. The journey had taken several hours, during which the children were silent, fearing the driver would kick them off if he discovered them. They were all thinking about what they saw in the sewer that morning. Although they had no proof, they knew that somehow that poor child died because of the Bonellis. They were free from St. Mary's dark dungeons. It was the first time the girls had seen clear skies and sunshine since leaving Brookings. A small herd of milk cows grazed in the adjacent pasture, and the foot of the Alps lay just a few miles beyond. A stone wall ran in front of the farm house and an old barn.

Giovanni was the first one out of the wagon after the driver made his way to the main farmhouse. He crouched behind the wall and peered over to see the driver greeted by a stout woman with open arms. The two embraced, kissing passionately. Peeking from the back of the van, Ilsa and the rest of the girls stared at the couple who pulled each other as close as possible. They seemed oblivious to all around them as they walked into the farmhouse. Clarissa let out a giggle and climbed out of the wagon. Heidi took a deep breath of the fresh air and the perfume of hay and grass. Seeing the cows and goats on the farm made Heidi smile; they reminded her of home. The group crawled along the outside of the wall until they were away from the front of the farmhouse. Making sure the couple weren't watching, Heidi led the children to the huge barn.

The barn was filled with stacks of hay and farm equipment. With the barn doors wide open, the children moved to the back of the building, looking for a hiding place. Giovanni opened a door at the far end of the stables. His eyes popped wide open when he saw what was inside the room. Food was everywhere. Buckets of fresh yogurt and kefir waiting to curdle stood in a row, welcoming their guests. Strands of mortadella salami and curing prosciutto hung from the rafters, almost waving the children inside. Wheels of pungent parmesan and romano cheese were stacked high, forming columns in the middle of the room. Rope-tied balls of mozzarella sat in a milky-white bath next to pans of sweet ricotta. An urn of fresh cream and milk was Giovanni's first target. He scooped up a handful of heavy top cream and slurped it up, giving himself a thick white moustache. The girls ran into the room grabbing at everything, helping themselves to the feast before them. Clarissa knelt by a bucket of yogurt and quickly looked up, mouthing the words, "Thank you." Then she put her entire face into the sweetly sour custard.

After tasting everything imaginable, the girls sat leaning against bales of hay in the main part of the barn, eating the apples Giovanni had found. Giovanni was out exploring the rest of the farm in search of more treasures.

"This is like a party, isn't it! I've never been to a party before," Clarissa said, happy to be with her new friends.

Ursula kept her eyes on the farmhouse, which she could see through the window. "We must go before they see us."

Clarissa giggled. "They can't see us. They're kissing."

"More like mashing their faces together," Ilsa said, hysterically laughing.

Clarissa thought about kissing. "What do they do with their teeth?" she tried kissing her own hand to see what it would be like. She pressed her lips against her knuckles and started giggling again. "It's really slippery." Heidi smiled. For the first time since they had left Brookings, her friends were laughing.

"The way he squeezed her, you'd think she wouldn't like it." Ilsa said, taking a more practical approach to the subject at hand. "Maybe we should watch some more."

"Really! This isn't a proper topic of conversation," Ursula insisted in her disapproving tone of voice.

"Why not, Ursula? They love each other," Heidi asked. Then, quietly, she said, "I have a friend. Peter. We love each other. We're best friends."

Gudron exclaimed, "You have a sweetheart!"

"Heidi's such a liar," Ursula told the girls.

"I know he loves me. He gave me this." Heidi took from her coat the pan pipes Peter had given her in Dörfli.

"Are you going to get married?" Ilsa asked.

"I don't know. He's very old. He's eighteen and he joined the army." Heidi thought of Peter in his new army uniform, saying good-bye to her in Dörfli.

"You're such a liar." Ursula spoke directly to Heidi, still nervous someone would see them.

"No she's not. Not if he gave her a present" said Clarissa, studying the pipes with great interest. "No one ever gave me . . ."

Suddenly a side door flew open! Bonelli stood holding Giovanni by the collar. Ilsa and Gudron screamed. Ursula

82

moved quickly to the the rest of the girls, who crouched behind Heidi.

"Naughty girls. You know you shouldn't have left Saint Mary's. We were so worried. Signora Bonelli is anxious to see you again. She hates curious children. Now, are we ready? You have work to do. A lot of work to do."

Giovanni grabbed a milking stool and slammed it into Bonelli's knees. Bonelli screamed in pain and dropped to the floor. "Run!" Giovanni shouted as he freed himself from Bonelli's grip.

The girls ran out the barn door, heading for the open space of the pasture. They ran as fast as their feet would carry them. Behind them was the devil. Giovanni only got to the barn doors before Bonelli had recovered and caught him. Bonelli got ahold of his arm and twisted it until he cried out. With one last gasp of energy, he kicked Bonelli in the shins, causing Bonelli to double over but not to lose his hold.

"Run. Run for your lives!" Giovanni shouted at his friends, knowing he would not escape.

The girls were halfway across the field before they realized Giovanni was not with them. "Where's Giovanni?" Clarissa screamed. She looked around. He was nowhere to be seen. Clarissa turned around to start back for her friend.

"No, Clarissa. No!" Heidi yelled. Clarissa wouldn't listen. As the other girls raced ahead, Heidi grabbed Clarissa, who kept trying to run back to the farm for Giovanni.

"He's my friend. Giovanni looked after me. We have to get him," she screamed.

Heidi didn't have time to argue. She scooped Clarissa up and ran after the other girls. "Maybe he got away," Heidi said to the sobbing little girl in her arms. But Heidi knew he had not. They had to escape. She caught up with the girls and dashed into the woods to safety. Above them towered the mighty Alps.

CHAPTER 8

The cold, winter fog swirled through the tops of the gnarled trees, shielding the approaching night. The ground pitched and turned, rocky and unforgiving, as Heidi led the exhausted Ursula, Ilsa, Gudron, and Clarissa through the pitted valley. Using all of her mountaineering skills, Heidi proceeded step by step, very much aware that a wrong turn could be disastrous. In the distance an orange light flashed through the sky every moment or two, followed by what sounded like thunder but was in reality heavy artillery. The girls were frightened and with reason, for they were unknowingly entering that deadly ground known as no-man's-land, the killing ground that separated armies.

It was now pitch dark. The girls were moving through a forest where the footing was extremely difficult under the best of circumstances when Heidi held up her hand for them to stop. Directly ahead of her was a narrow opening, most likely made by a deer, thought Heidi, in a dense thicket which offered some hope of shelter. Heidi knew it was impossible to continue; they were hopelessly lost, and exhausted and frightened. Motioning for the others to follow her, Heidi led them through the opening into a small clearing in the middle of the thicket. It would have to do.

"We'll stay here until morning," Heidi told them. The girls huddled together for warmth. Clarissa was whimpering.

"What are we doing in this godforsaken place anyway?" Ursula directed the question at all of them. Ilsa had already fallen asleep while Heidi attempted to comfort Clarissa. Gudron was preoccupied with staying warm, but Heidi looked up from the frightened orphan she held in her arms and looked directly at Ursula. There was a challenging look in Heidi's eyes; she was determined not to let this opportunity pass. Through those difficult days at Brookings, and again at the orphanage, Ursula had made Heidi's life miserable.

"Trying to stay alive, Ursula, . . . that's what we're trying to do, so I suggest you get some sleep."

Ursula was very frightened. The orphanage was bad, but at least there she knew where she was.

"I told you we should have waited for Mrs. Hillary," Ursula responded.

All Heidi could do was shake her head. "Go to sleep, Ursula."

Juliet Caton as Heidi.

Charlie Sheen as Peter.

Jan Rubes as Grandfather.

Peter knows it is time to leave the peaceful world of the Alm.

Heidi and Peter pass through Dörfli, leaving their home for the first time.

Faced with the loss of Brookings, Mrs. Hillary comforts the girls.

Heidi gathers her courage for the dangerous glacier crossing.

Signor Bonelli, the ruthless orphanage administrator, plots to foil Heidi's plan.

Signor Bonelli forces Heidi and the girls across the Alps.

Grandfather entrusts Peter with the task of rescuing Heidi.

Peter surveys the glacier before embarking on his perilous mission.

Mrs. Hillary and Grandfather hear the call of the ram's horn.

Heidi and Grandfather, joyfully reunited.

———

The sound was horrific. The screams of horses in pain and of wounded men in agony and the crash of caissons and cannons careening through the dark forest announced the beginning of the battle. Men's curses mixed with the rhythmic chatter of machine guns and the staccato of rifle fire. Worst of all was the deafening roar of the artillery. Barrage after barrage filled the air, first from one side, then from the other. It was night, yet the sky flashed white and seemed to bounce across the heavens. The ground literally jumped with each barrage; trees leaped upward in clouds of dirt, while debris and deadly shrapnel scattered in all directions. For the moment, still hidden in their forest thicket, Heidi and the girls could only hold their ears and pray. Logic told them they were smack in the middle of some battle, but they were sure they were already in hell.

Mrs. Hillary's horse-drawn taxi slowly made its way down one of Tirano's most prestigious streets. But on this particular wintry evening the street was hardly prestigious, for it was lined with battle-weary soldiers marching back from the front. They filled the street, too tired to care about the horse-drawn ambulance vans and the few commercial vehicles pounding along the pavement. Mrs. Hillary's taxi pulled up in front of a luxurious town house set back from the street. A doorman was instantly at the taxi to greet the expected guest of his employer, the Governor of Tirano.

Another liveried servant escorted Mrs. Hillary through

the foyer, which was crammed with expensive furnishings. It appeared to Mrs. Hillary, as she marched behind the blue-and-gold-clad servant, that this was more of a warehouse than the elegant home that its architecture demanded. The servant stopped before a beautifully carved mahogany door and graciously opened it for Mrs. Hillary, who gasped when she saw the governor standing behind her own desk! The governor, large, proud as a peacock, and beaming, motioned her inside.

"That's my desk!" exclaimed Mrs. Hillary.

"Of course it is, Signora, and I am proud to have it in my home. I believe you have already met my aide-de-camp, Major Rieti, and my guests, Signor and Signora Bonelli."

Mrs. Hillary turned to her right. There near the large marble fireplace stood the three people she hated most in the world. Without acknowledging them, Mrs. Hillary turned back to the governor.

"I'm not going to mince words, Governor, and I assure you that with regard to my property, that matter will be dealt with by my solicitor in due course. But right now, I hold you responsible for my students that under your order were sent to the state orphanage . . . or I should say, state prison. I demand you order this creature to release them at once."

The governor was furious. How dare this foreigner make demands to the Governor of Tirano. "Preposterous! We are at war, Signora. My soldiers are now bleeding on our very streets." The governor dramatically gestured toward the window. "And you demand I release children from a safe and honorable institution to be let loose when we are under siege from the Austrians. Preposterous!"

"How can I know they are even alive, your Excellency, in the care of these two monsters?" Mrs. Hillary said in utter desperation.

The governor saw that Mrs. Hillary was a determined woman. He could not afford to have her running to Rome with all kinds of wild exaggerations. "Signora Hillary. Calm yourself. I will tell you what I will do. We will go to Saint Mary's, where you can see the girls for a short visit. And that will be the end of it." The governor was impressed with his unique gift of solving problems.

Signor Bonelli gave her husband a jab with her elbow and literally pushed him toward the center of the room.

"Forgive me, your Excellency, but the children in question are no longer at Saint Mary's," Signor Bonelli stuttered.

The governor's jaw dropped. This he was not prepared for, and his face soon glowed like red heat. Mrs. Hillary gasped, then strode the few feet to the quivering Bonelli.

"And where are they?" she exclaimed.

"Exactly, Bonelli, where are they?" demanded the governor.

Signora Bonelli stepped to her husband's side. "They have run away, your Excellency. I tried to reassure them that they would not have to go back to this woman, but the silly girls were petrified that somehow Mrs. Hillary, whom they hated, your Excellency, would soon have them back." Signora Bonelli oozed.

"This is totally ridiculous, and a bold-faced lie!" exclaimed Mrs. Hillary.

The governor also knew it was a lie, but at the moment

he had no choice except to support the Bonellis. "Mrs. Hillary, this is indeed unfortunate. I can only say that every effort will be made to bring the children back to Saint Mary's." The governor turned to his aide-de-camp. "Major Rieti, you will assist Signor Bonelli in this matter. I want those little girls found as soon as possible."

"Yes, your Excellency," the major responded.

Mrs. Hillary eyed the governor. She understood only too well the game that was being played. "Governor, as I said earlier, I hold you responsible for the safety of my girls. I will lodge a formal complaint through the consulate here in Tirano and with the British ambassador in Rome. I assure you this matter will be treated most seriously by your government, and even more so if the children are not handed over to me after they are found. Good day."

Giving the governor a stern look and totally dismissing the major and the Bonellis, Mrs. Hillary turned on her heel, head held high, and exited the study. There was a hushed silence in the room. The governor was already calculating the repercussions from Rome, and needless to say, he was not happy.

"Imbeciles! You three are responsible for this trouble, and for what? Some furniture, most of which I will have to keep in storage. As for the estate, we easily could have taken it after the army left."

The major gathered his courage. He had looked after this man for many years and he was not about to be made the scapegoat for this sordid affair.

"Your Excellency, with all due respect, may I remind you that legally we had to have possession of Brookings before the army took it over. I signed the property over to the army for the duration of the siege; otherwise it would have been Mrs. Hillary's. We had to take possession that night."

The governor reflected on this. The major was clever and had made him a good deal of money over the years. He was usually right when it came to circumventing the law. The governor turned to the cowering Bonellis. Here was another matter.

"And you two wanted Brookings for your own school, yes . . . ?" the governor purred. "Our arrangement was for me to take over the property and lease it to you. We would keep the soap factory going and you would have your private school, paying me a handsome sum for the use of the land and buildings. And now you have put all of that in jeopardy. How will you have your school now, if what goes on at Saint Mary's comes to light?" The governor paused to catch his breath.

"Not just a school. It would be the finest private school in Europe, all for the glory of the state and in your name," argued Bonelli. Signora Bonelli nodded in agreement.

"Such noble thoughts," the governor said sarcastically. "Let me make myself clear. In all probability there will be an investigation ordered from Rome. Not right away, but soon. Your orphanage is a pig pen, and I want it cleaned up and the children decently fed and clothed. You will take the money for the expenses from your share of the soap profits, and if the Brookings girls are found, and let us pray they are not, I will have no other choice now but to give them over to Mrs. Hillary. Now, get going! I will personally conduct an inspection of Saint Mary's in three days."

Signora and Signor Bonelli, muttering to themselves, walked briskly down the long corridor toward the front door. Signora Bonelli looked carefully about to be certain they were not being observed. Satisfied that they were alone, she pulled her husband close to her.

"We are finished if the major finds the girls before we do. They have seen the sewer, so you know what that means. If you hadn't let them get away at that dairy farm, we wouldn't be in this mess. You must find them first, and then arrange an accident . . . a fatal accident. Do you understand me, my husband?" Signor Bonelli slowly nodded his head. He knew what was at stake and what he must do.

Smoke drifted through the burnt forest, caressing and silent as it moved, enveloping all before it. The battlefield was deserted; all that remained from the previous night of terror were the twisted shapes of trees, horses, wagons, and men left in death. It was quiet except for the faint cries from those few soldiers who had been left to die.

Heidi led her soot-covered band from what remained of their thicket onto the smoke-filled battlefield. There was nowhere else to go. The sights and smells of the aftermath were horrific, causing the shell-shocked girls to cover their eyes whenever possible. They tramped forward through the ashes, avoiding the bodies of the fallen soldiers and horses, following Heidi.

"Are they Italians or Austrians?" asked Ursula in a shaking voice.

"It doesn't matter," Heidi answered.

Heidi's only thought was to somehow get them away from the hell that surrounded them, and to do this, she kept moving upward through the foothills. She knew that the higher they got, the closer they would be to her beloved mountains. They struggled on for over an hour, always upward, and yet the remnants of the battle were still all about them. The girls wanted to stop and rest, but Heidi kept them moving, determined to reach the high ground and to get away from the stench and horror of the battlefield. She reminded herself over and over again of the clean, sweet air of the Alps—somewhere up there, ahead of them, was Switzerland. It had to be, unless her sense of direction was completely off. Ursula whined that she couldn't go on, but Heidi refused to listen. She led them upward through a grove of shattered fir trees, which apparently had been heavily defended, for there were bodies everywhere. Once they had passed through the grove, the girls climbed a small hill on which flew a tattered Italian flag marking, Heidi thought, some kind of command post. Here, the air was mostly clear of the smoke and Heidi could look down across the miles of torn and battered earth they had come from. Ilsa stood looking in the opposite direction, up, toward the sky, and slowly pointed. "Heidi, look!"

Heidi turned and gasped, for there in all its splendor, rising directly above her, was her mountain. The girls clustered around her, admiring the snow-clad, majestic peak. "On the other side of that mountain is Switzerland . . . and the Alm, my home."

"Is that where we're going, Heidi?" asked Clarissa.

Heidi turned back to face the girls. She had made up her mind, but what about her friends, whom she now felt responsible for? Could she ask them to make what she knew would be a difficult and dangerous journey? "The only other choice we have is to go back down, see if we can find a town where we could send a telegram." Heidi said.

"I'm not going back down there," Gudron exclaimed. Heidi looked at Ursula, who was biting her lip, trying to make up her mind. She was afraid of the mountain, but she was even more afraid of facing those staring, empty faces again at St. Mary's.

Clarissa reached for Heidi's hand. "I want to go to Switzerland with Heidi."

Heidi squeezed Clarissa's hand and smiled. "All right then, Ursula, what about you?" Ursula looked down the hill, toward the carnage they had just walked through, and made up her mind.

"Switzerland. . . . But I need shoes."

Heidi thought about this for a moment. It was true, if they were going to make the climb over the mountain they were going to need many things, and there was only one place to find them. Taking a deep breath, she started toward the command post. The girls followed her, not knowing quite what to expect. On reaching the first dead soldier, Heidi bent down and pulled his blanket from his pack, then began to unbuckle the pack harness itself.

"All of you, find blankets, food, any warm clothing, anything you think we might need up there." Heidi continued to struggle with the harness as the girls moved through the deserted post, hesitant but knowing what they had to do. Ilsa picked up a blanket roll while Gudron found a haversack packed with food leaning against a tree. Ursula stood looking down at the young face before her, at the eyes staring at her. She was transfixed. Heidi, with the backpack now strapped on her back, came up beside Ursula. Realizing what was happening, Heidi knelt beside the dead soldier and removed his knife, then gently turned the body over in order to remove his pack. She handed the pack to Ursula and set off to find the other girls.

On a nearby hill, a young Italian officer carefully scanned the surrounding hills through his binoculars. A movement caught his eye and he quickly refocused the binoculars. At first he couldn't believe what he was seeing, but, yes, there were five girls, all dressed in varying bits and pieces of army clothing and equipment, marching in single file straight toward the Swiss border. The startled officer quickly reached for the nearby field telephone.

CHAPTER 9

A bitterly cold wind swept down the mountain, whipping the tall fir trees and sending small rocks cascading down the slope. Shielding their faces as best they could, the five girls struggled up the steep incline. They had been climbing steadily for over six hours since they had left the battlefield. As the sun began to set, Heidi signaled the girls to halt.

"We have to find some kind of shelter. This storm is only going to get worse. Let's try up there." Heidi pointed to a small grove of trees on a narrow shelf of rock directly above them. The girls looked at where they would have to climb and shook their heads.

"We can't go up there," moaned Gudron.

Realizing that she would have to make the climb alone, Heidi started up the sheer face of rock, carefully choosing each foothold as she inched her way painfully upward. Her right foot slipped, but Heidi held on for dear life, desperately trying to regain her foothold. Ursula screamed. Feeling her foot finally in place, Heidi put her weight on it and pushed upward, clawing for the top until she had a firm grip. Heidi pulled herself up bit by bit until she was over the face of the cliff and safely on the sheltered ledge. The girls below waved and cheered. Heidi reached into her pack and withdrew a length of rope, which she tied around a tree.

"I'm going to throw this rope down to you. Clarissa, I want you to go first, then Ilsa, Gudron, and finally Ursula. You hold on to it and simply walk up the slope, moving your hands forward on the rope," Heidi shouted. She threw the rope down, and when Ursula had caught it Heidi tested that her end was securely tied to the tree. Down below, Clarissa, scared to death but determined she would at least try, grabbed the rope and started up the face of the cliff. She found that once she found the rhythm of moving her hands forward, it was relatively easy. In moments she was in Heidi's arms.

"I did it! Come on Ilsa, it's fun," Clarissa shouted down the cliff.

After Ilsa and Gudron had scaled the cliff without mishap, it was Ursula's turn. Heidi threw the rope to her, but Ursula was far too frightened to pick it up, let alone try to climb the cliff. Being the oldest girl, she was embarrassed; but she was still determined not to make the climb. Heidi instinctively knew there was not a chance of talking her into it from where she was; Ursula needed help and quickly, before she completely panicked. Taking up the rope, Heidi easily moved down the cliff to where Ursula waited.

"You're not going to make me go up there!" Ursula cried. The storm was getting stronger, and it was now difficult for both girls to keep their footing on the narrow trail. There wasn't much time and Heidi knew it.

"Ursula, I'm not going to make you do anything you don't want to, but we can't stay here. Neither can we go back down in this storm. It's only going to get worse." Heidi spoke calmly. Ursula started to cry. She didn't know what to do.

"We're going to do this together. I'll be right behind you and we'll be up there before you know it." Heidi reached for Ursula's hand, but Ursula shook her head. She couldn't do it. A strong gust of wind sent Ursula tumbling into Heidi, who reacted by taking advantage of the moment, getting Ursula to grab hold of the rope. It was now or never.

"We're going to walk right to the top. Don't look down and just keep moving!" Pushing Ursula ahead of her, Heidi started up the face of the cliff. Shouting words of encouragement and pulling with all her strength, Heidi was able to get them nearly to the ledge.

Then Ursula opened her eyes and froze. "Heidi, I can't do it! We're going to fall!" she screamed.

"No! Keep climbing, we're almost there!" Heidi shouted. Knowing she had no other option, Heidi pushed with all her might, sending Ursula over the top, where Ilsa, Gudron, and Clarissa pulled the screaming girl to safety. Heidi dangled precariously on the face of the cliff, the wind pounding her against the rocky surface, until she was able to control the rope and her upward movement. As she reached the sheltered shelf, the girls were able to get a secure hold and pulled her over the top. Winded, Heidi looked around at the anxious faces. Even Ursula was concerned.

"I'm all right. . . . Start collecting pine boughs for beds. It will be dark soon and very cold tonight." Ilsa, Gudron, and Clarissa immediately moved to do her bidding, leaving Ursula and Heidi alone.

"It wasn't so bad now, was it?" Heidi asked.

All Ursula could do was stare at Heidi. She still couldn't believe what had happened. "It was awful, and I hate you for bringing us here." Ursula turned and stalked off to join the other girls, leaving a very perplexed Heidi.

Heidi built a small fire, which she surrounded with rocks in order to provide more heat. Although the wind had died down, the night was very cold, as Heidi had predicted. The girls clustered about the fire with their blankets wrapped around them, attempting to keep warm, but except for Heidi, who was used to the mountains, they were not having much success. Gudron was actually shaking with cold.

"If it's this cold here, what's it going to be like farther up the mountain?" Ilsa asked Heidi, who was now rubbing Gudron's hands. Heidi shook her head. She knew the girls were miserable, but if they could just get through the next couple of days, they would at least become more acclimated to the weather.

"Well, it certainly isn't going to be warmer, is it." Heidi replied.

"That's comforting," mumbled Gudron. "I don't think I've ever been so cold. Heidi, maybe we should go back down? I don't want to freeze to death up there." Heidi measured each girl in turn. Ursula was sullen and defiant; Ilsa and Gudron were just cold; and Clarissa snuggled up to Heidi with a smile that simply said "I'll go where you go."

"You're not going to freeze to death, none of you are, not if you listen to me and do what I tell you. I know it won't be easy, but it's better than going back to the orphanage, and that's what I'm afraid of if we go back down. I don't know how you all feel, but I doubt Bonelli has given up." Heidi threw two more logs onto the flames and they quickly caught, warming the girls. "Now, let's try and get some sleep. The pine boughs will help you keep warm. Just don't get them too close to the fire."

As the girls arranged themselves, Heidi put a few more rocks around the fire. She didn't know what the others were going to do the next morning, but she was determined to go on. She thought Clarissa and Ilsa would go with her, but she wasn't that sure about Gudron. And as for Ursula, Heidi thought, well, if she wanted to go back, let her. Snuggling down into her own bed of pine boughs, Heidi pulled her blanket tightly around her. Looking up into the night sky, she could barely make out in the darkness the shapes of the clouds moving above her. It was as if they were on some mission, she thought. Propelled by the wind, heading south toward Tirano, the clouds were like her soldiers, imagined Heidi, going to strike her enemies. They would stand between her and the Bonellis; her soldiers from the Alm would never let her and her friends be captured. Heidi smiled. How wonderful fantasy was. Somehow up on this mountain it all seemed possible. Her last thoughts as she drifted off to sleep were of Grandfather and Peter.

Mrs. Hillary couldn't believe her eyes. Her beloved Brookings and its beautiful gardens were literally covered with soldiers and horses going this way and that, and trucks were tearing a new road in what was once the vast front lawn. She stifled a cry and let a young officer lead her toward one of the command tents. She saw that the mansion itself appeared to have been turned into a hospital, judging from the ambulances that were unloading their battered, half-dead victims. Those who had already been treated were stretched out on simple bedrolls near the east wing, row after row of them. These were the ones who were just waiting to die, the lieutenant told her. There wasn't any more room for them inside. Asking her if she would kindly wait for a moment, the officer disappeared into a tent. Mrs. Hillary was amazed at the callousness of the lieutenant: "There isn't room for them inside anymore." No sign of pity or compassion; this was war, was what he was implying. He didn't have time for the dying, Mrs. Hillary sadly reflected. How could such a civilized country as Italy, let alone England, France, Germany, and Austria, ever believe that war was justified? She knew that millions had already been killed; God only knew how many more would die before this was all over.

"Ridiculous," Mrs. Hillary said out loud.

"I beg your pardon, Signora."

Mrs. Hillary whirled to find Captain Ornesco addressing her. "Oh, Captain. . . . I'm sorry, it was just . . . You wanted to see me?"

"My apologies, Signora, for you having to come all the way out here, but as you can see, we are rather busy." Mrs. Hillary was not amused at his choice of words, which by her gesture the captain easily surmised. "I am sorry. To the point then, it was reported late yesterday by one of our field observation posts north of here that they spotted five young ladies above the foothills, climbing toward the Bernina glacier. They must be your girls."

At first Mrs. Hillary could only stare at him, trying to comprehend the meaning of his words. "My God, they're alive!" she cried.

"Is there anything I can do, Signora?"

Without a moment's pause, Mrs. Hillary had made a decision. "Thank you, Captain. You can help me arrange a cable to the grandfather of one of the girls, and provide me with a pass to cross your lines into Switzerland."

Here was a very stubborn woman, thought Captain Ornesco. He smiled. "Not another international incident, Signora Hillary?" There was a long pause as the two measured each other, then Mrs. Hillary shook her head.

"My general will be pleased to make the necessary arrangements. I will meet you at your hotel in two hours.

Good day." The captain clicked his heels, turned, and reentered the command tent.

Mrs. Hillary, looking neither right nor left, walked at a brisk pace to where she had left her automobile. She failed to see the governor's aide-de-camp, Major Rieti, standing to one side of the command tent. It was obvious from the satisfied look on his face that he had overheard the entire conversation between Mrs. Hillary and the gallant captain.

The early-morning sun was a pleasant change from the storm and bitter cold. Heidi had found a small goat trail where the going was much easier than on the preceding day. They were still climbing, but not straight up as before. Heidi noted that the girls were in much better spirits and there had not been one word about going back down the mountain, even from Ursula. They reached a high mountain meadow where four wild goats were grazing, and Heidi signaled the girls to be quiet.

"We'll stop here for a rest, and I'll see if I can get us some milk. Everyone be very quiet; we don't want to scare the goats," Heidi whispered.

The girls settled into the tall alpine grass and carefully studied the goats, who warily kept an eye on their new guests. Carefully slipping her pack off, Heidi removed a canteen and then quietly stood up. One of the goats gave Heidi a suspicious look, but after a thorough inspection he decided the figure before him was not dangerous and so returned to his grazing. Heidi took three more steps toward the goats, then stopped. This time all four goats raised their heads. Making the same soothing sounds she had used with her own Schwanli and with Peter's goats, Heidi advanced a few more yards. Still the goats didn't move. Somehow they knew this person was a friend and could be trusted. After a moment, Heidi moved to where the closest goat was grazing. She knew exactly what she wanted and tenderly petted her behind the ear.

The girls were amazed at Heidi's success. As they watched, the remaining three goats came to Heidi to be petted.

"How does she do it?" Ilsa wondered.

"If I tried that, those goats would still be running," Clarissa exclaimed.

"Silly, Heidi has lived with goats. Couldn't you smell her when she first came to Brookings? Who wants to drink goat's milk anyway? Certainly not me," Ursula countered.

Gudron made a face at her. "Why are you so mean, Ursula, were you born that way or what?" Before Ursula could respond, Ilsa pointed toward Heidi. "Look, she wants us to join her. She's actually milking that goat. Come on." Ilsa was on her feet and started toward Heidi, walking deliberately, the way she had seen her friend do. She was quickly followed by Gudron and Clarissa, but not Ursula. She wouldn't budge.

The giggling girls watched Heidi as she delicately milked the goat, filling the canteen to the brim. When she finished, Heidi petted the goat as if to say thank you and took the canteen to her three friends.

"All right, who wants to be first?" Heidi said. However, the girls were not too sure, not having tasted goat's milk before. "Here, I'll show you." Heidi drank from the canteen. "It's delicious. . . . Come on, don't be silly."

Clarissa stepped timidly forward and Heidi let her drink from the canteen. First a sip, measuring the taste, then a big smile from Clarissa. "It's good. . . . It really is" Clarissa gave the canteen to Ilsa and Gudron, and they were as surprised as Clarissa had been.

"Now, who wants to learn how to milk a goat?" Heidi asked. "It's really easy."

"How do you know how?" Clarissa wanted to know.

"I grew up with my own pet goat that Grandfather gave me. Her name is Schwanli."

"I want to meet Schwanli," said Clarissa.

Giving the canteen back to Heidi, Ilsa looked thoughtfully at the goat Heidi had just milked. "It won't kick, will it?"

Heidi smiled and shook her head. She led Ilsa over to the goat and showed the girl how to pet her. The goat nuzzled Ilsa. Kneeling beside the goat, Heidi showed Ilsa exactly what she had to do, and after a few tries Ilsa was milking her first goat. Heidi looked up and saw Ursula standing nearby. "Do you want to try, Ursula?"

Wetting her lips, Ursula was tempted. "Not right now; maybe later. I thought we could talk?" Turning to the girls, Heidi told them to keep on practicing and to fill up their own canteens if they could.

The two older girls walked along a small mountain stream that ran down through the meadow from one of the many mountain glaciers. Heidi and Ursula were absorbed in the beauty around them, thinking their own thoughts but both wondering what the next few days would bring.

"Do you honestly believe you can get us over that mountain and into Switzerland?" Ursula quietly asked. Heidi looked up at the mountain that towered above them, then back at Ursula. Heidi was confident; some inner knowledge told her she could do it. She nodded her head affirmatively.

"I really think we should go back and try to find Mrs. Hillary, but I've been thinking about what you said about Mr. Bonelli. I couldn't stand another moment in that orphanage." Ursula studied the mountain for a moment. "I've never done anything like this before, and I'm frightened."

"I'm not going to lie to you, Ursula. It isn't going to be easy, like it was today." Heidi said.

"No, that's what I'm afraid of. But still, it does seem like the sensible thing to do once you think about it. . . . So, how long do you think it will take us?" The girls were standing on a small knoll, looking toward the meadow where Clarissa, Gudron, and Ilsa were still playing with the goats. Heidi and Ursula could hear their laughter. Heidi smiled.

"They're having such a good time. . . ." She turned to Ursula, very serious. "Three or four days. It will depend on the weather. On a day like today we should be climbing, but we also needed the goats' milk."

"And we needed to talk," Ursula said. She strode toward the other girls at the bottom of the meadow. Heidi watched her and wondered whether she had won Ursula over. Somehow, she doubted it.

106

CHAPTER 10

The Piz Bernina border post, which separated Switzerland and Italy, consisted of several buildings bedecked with the two countries' flags along with the traditional red-and-white-striped barrier pole. This particular post was responsible for civilians crossing the border on foot, by horse and mule caravans, and lately in the odd automobile. The train crossing was farther down the valley. Mrs. Hillary showed her papers to the Swiss Border Patrol officer, who politely waved her on. At his signal the barrier pole was raised, and Mrs. Hillary released the clutch of the touring car. The next moment she was in Switzerland. Despite the beauty of the Alps directly in front of her, literally sparkling in the sun, Mrs. Hillary's only thoughts were of her girls and of getting to Dörfli as soon as possible.

Outfitted in his recently purchased alpine climbing gear, Signor Bonelli conferred with the senior guide of the Italian Alpine Mountain Station near the Piz Bernina Pass. On having been informed by Major Rieti of the children's whereabouts and that they indeed intended to cross over into Switzerland, the Bonellis knew their only chance of survival was to make certain the children were never heard from again. As far as the governor was concerned, he was happy to be rid of the children. Let them stay in Switzerland. But not Signora and Signor Bonelli. If the children did reach Dörfli and told their story of what they had seen in the sewers beneath St. Mary's, the Bonellis were finished. The guide showed Bonelli on the map exactly where the children had last been seen as well as the route they would probably have to take to cross the mountain to Dörfli.

"I can spare only one guide and a pack mule, Signor Bonelli, but since I realize time is of the essence, you would be better off forgetting the mule." Signor Bonelli scanned the mountain with his binoculars. He had no thought of taking either the guide or the pack mule.

"I thank you for your offer, but as you say, time is everything if I am to save these unfortunate little ones. I have climbed these same mountains many times and would be able to make better time on my own." The guide shrugged, knowing Bonelli was foolish; but he had dealt with many bureaucrats in the past and was not very surprised.

"As you wish. Good luck." The senior guide turned and returned to his outpost, leaving Bonelli to begin his search.

Heidi surveyed the gorge with some misgivings. The only crossing for miles was a narrow rope suspension bridge and it didn't appear too sturdy, being in obvious disrepair. Yet, Heidi knew, it would take them at least two more days if they tried to follow the gorge and cross farther down the mountain. She turned back to the girls, who were not happy about using the bridge.

"Look, we don't have much of a choice. I'm going to try it first. I want you to wait here. Take your ropes out and tie them together. Ursula will help you." Without waiting for a reply from Ursula or the other girls, Heidi made her way the short distance to the bridge. She carefully checked the ropes on her side of the gorge, which were each tied around a tree. Finding that one of the suspension ropes was frayed, Heidi replaced it with her own, which she had been carrying coiled over her shoulder. The gorge dropped several hundred feet to a raging river below. Knowing not to look down, Heidi started across the bridge, cautiously testing each plank as she went. Halfway across, several planks were missing. Grabbing hold of the outside ropes that served as a railing, Heidi pulled herself forward over the empty space left by the missing planks. Upon reaching the other side of the gorge, Heidi searched desperately for anything to replace the planks. She knew the girls couldn't cross otherwise. Finding a bushy fir tree near the bridge, Heidi began cutting the lower branches. She gathered up as many as she could carry and started back for the bridge.

After Heidi had laid the branches over the empty space, crisscrossing them in order to provide firmer footing, she gingerly tested the new section. Satisfied that it would hold, she called out to the girls.

"All right . . . Ursula, take the long rope and tie a loop around yourself, Gudron, Ilsa, and Clarissa. Make sure that the loop is tied as tightly as you can, and keep as much rope as possible with you. . . . Coil it like I showed you. Do you understand?"

Ursula slowly nodded her head. She was too frightened to do anything but what Heidi told her to do. There was no time to think, complain, or argue or they would never get across the gorge. After tying each girl securely so that they were connected, Ursula coiled what was left of the rope and waved to Heidi on the other side of the gorge.

"Good, Ursula, I want you to come first. Have the others keep the rope between each girl as taut as possible. When you come to the bridge, throw me the coiled rope," Heidi instructed.

Ursula hesitated for only a moment. Saying a silent prayer, she started for the bridge, towing in their proper order, Gudron, Ilsa, and Clarissa behind her. Each girl swallowed several times. They all knew this wasn't going to be easy. Heidi, in the meantime, again tested the new planking. It would have to do.

When Ursula reached the bridge she threw the coiled rope she held in front of her to Heidi, who, keeping the rope taut, carefully backed along the bridge to the opposite side from Ursula and the girls. Tying the rope around the fir tree from which she had taken the branches, Heidi retraced her steps to the bridge and took hold of the rope.

"Ursula, all of you. . . . Come across slowly, holding onto the side ropes, and whatever you do, don't look down! I will be pulling from this side."

Ursula looked back at Gudron, Ilsa, and Clarissa. They were all scared to death, but each was willing to try. "All right?" Ursula asked. Gudron, who was second in line, smiled weakly. "No, Ursula, not all right, but let's go."

As Ursula led the way across the bridge, Heidi took up the slack on the rope. Slowly, ever so slowly, the girls moved along the swaying rope bridge, saying to themselves over and over again their favorite prayer. Being the first to cross, Ursula helped Heidi with the rope until Gudron and Ilsa were across. Then, Clarissa looked down and screamed. She froze, resisting the rope, and screamed at the top of her voice.

"Quickly, pull her in!" Heidi commanded. With a jerk, Clarissa was across and sobbing in Heidi's arms. "It's all right, Clarissa. You're safe now." Clarissa looked up into Heidi's face and knew that everything was indeed all right.

The Swiss barracks was strategically located on the eastern side of the Bernina Pass, facing the Italians to the south and the Austrians slightly to the north. It was garrisoned with a full company of crack alpine troops who were rotated every three months to Sils Maria.

Grandfather was allowed to pass through the main gate and told to wait in the nearby orderly room. Warming his hands over the coal-burning central stove, Grandfather once again went over in his mind the contents of the telegram he had received only hours before. It was dated two days ago from a certain Italian captain whose name Grandfather couldn't remember, saying that Mrs. Hillary had instructed him to pass on the information that his granddaughter and four other girls were apparently attempting to cross over the Bernina Pass from Italy.

Peter entered the room to face a very concerned and weary old man. Grandfather reached into his coat pocket and shoved the telegram at Peter.

"It's about Heidi. She and some other children are trying to cross the pass." Peter couldn't believe what he was hearing. Shaking his head, he scanned the short telegram.

"This is insane. Coming from Italy, they'll have to cross the glacier," Peter exclaimed. The two men could only stare at each other, both knowing only too well the dangers that could befall Heidi and the others. Grandfather cleared his throat; this was very difficult for him. Before him stood not the boy who always used to be underfoot but a young man.

"Peter, can you help?" Grandfather said quietly. "I would go, but I no longer have the strength."

Peter's mind raced back to the many times he had seen this man, whom he had revered all his life, carrying stacks of hardwood that no ordinary man could even lift. He might not be as strong as he once was, Peter thought, but Grandfather was here asking him for the first time to do something important. Peter was in peak condition, and being entrusted with a vital mission. Army or no army, he wasn't going to let this man down. He was certain that the lieutenant would let him go—and if not, he would go anyway.

"Don't worry, Grandfather. I'll find them. You go back to Dörfli. The telegram says that this Mrs. Hillary is on her way there." Peter put his arm around Grandfather and walked him to the door. "I'll leave within the hour," Peter said.

Grandfather's eyes said all there was to say. He extended his hand to Peter, and then he was gone.

The narrow goat trail stretched up and up and the going was extremely difficult as Heidi led the girls ever upward over the rocky ground. The girls were nearing exhaustion; even Clarissa was moaning, and Ursula could barely walk. A blister had developed on Ursula's heel and the pain was severe. Upon reaching the top of the ridge, Heidi told them to rest. The girls collapsed where they were standing, too tired even to notice what lay directly ahead of them, the formidable Bernina glacier. It stretched for miles, towering fields of ice of various shades of blue, beautiful and deadly. Gazing out onto the glacier, Heidi took a deep breath, knowing the most difficult part of their journey was before them.

"You don't expect us to cross that, do you?" whispered Ursula. She was standing next to Heidi, holding her battered shoe. Looking at the monstrous mountains of ice, Ursula shuddered. She was certain that if she stepped onto that surface she would simply disappear.

"There are safe trails through the ice that the goats have made. Peter told me."

All Ursula could do was shake her head back and forth, back and forth. Tears were pouring down her face. "No, Heidi, I can't. I can't even walk; the blister has burst."

113

Gudron, Ilsa, and Clarissa, now very much aware of the imposing glacier, had formed a circle around the two older girls. They instinctively knew they were witnessing some kind of crisis that would affect all of them.

Heidi reached out to Ursula, who stepped back. "No, I have to go back. . . . You . . . don't understand. . . . None of you understand."

Heidi knew she had to remain calm and that everything depended on her retaining control. She didn't know exactly what was happening here, but she realized it was serious. "Ursula, once we cross the glacier—and I promise you I'll get you across safely—we're almost there. Dörfli couldn't be more than a few hours' walk down the mountain. Then, Grandfather can notify your parents."

Ursula heard the words. She knew what they meant. Something about Heidi's grandfather notifying her parents . . . yes, her parents. Ursula laughed. But she could see by the puzzled look on Heidi's face that she didn't understand. Ursula could feel that the rage and hatred, steadily building inside her for all these years, were about to burst. She clamped her mouth shut. No, she wasn't going to let it out. But it was too late.

"I don't have any parents!" Ursula screamed. "I have no one except Mrs. Hillary, and she's left me, hasn't she . . . up here to freeze to death!" The girls were stunned. Ursula was now hysterical. "Yes, I don't have a father or a mother! They took her away; it wasn't proper, they said, for her to have me. She was too young. Don't you understand . . . ?" Ursula cried. "The school was my home. There's no one else. I'm alone!"

114

There was a hush as Heidi, Gudron, Ilsa, and Clarissa grasped what they had just been told. They still couldn't believe it. However, it now made so much sense, Heidi thought, all that hurt. Heidi's heart went out to the poor girl.

"That isn't true, Ursula. You have us," Heidi said. She took a step toward Ursula, then stopped. "If you want you can live with me and Grandfather."

"Or you can live with us. We have a big house, and even an older brother," Ilsa added. "And I have a sister who is married that can tell you all about men," Gudron said with a smile. The girls surrounded Ursula, and Heidi gave her a big hug.

"I'll try, Heidi," was all Ursula could manage to reply.

CHAPTER 11

Signor Bonelli methodically swept the mountain with his binoculars. He could barely make out the beginning of the glacier several hundred feet above him. There were no signs of the children, but he was sure he was not far behind them, as he had made very good time. Being an experienced climber gave him a distinct advantage. He had come across the remnants of one of their camps earlier that morning. They were up there all right; it was now only a matter of time, which he was convinced had turned in his favor. Feeling very confident, Signor Bonelli set off at a brisk pace up the mountain trail.

Heidi led the girls through the jagged fields of ice, checking the area in front of her carefully with the long pole she had cut before they had started across the glacier.

Remembering what Peter had taught her, she was making sure the ice was solid underfoot. Only an hour before, one side of the trail had simply disappeared down the mountain when she had tested it with her pole. She shuddered to think what would have happened if she hadn't checked that section of ice. The going was slow and painful for all of them; the rough ice had practically shredded what was left of their shoes. Heidi had the girls cut pieces from their army blankets and wrap them around their feet, which helped for a short while. Heidi was aware that their next problem might be frostbite. She checked for storm clouds and was relieved that none were in sight. Right then, a storm would be the worst thing that could happen to them. Heidi sighed. All she could think of was getting across the glacier and down the other side of the mountain to Grandfather and Peter. She never wanted to leave the Alm ever again.

Ursula, last in the line, could barely concentrate on just putting one foot in front of the other, the pain was so bad. But she hadn't complained, and she knew that, somehow, she was going to get through all this. What her future would be Ursula didn't know, except that she was going to find Mrs. Hillary. As she had told Heidi and the others, Brookings was the only home she had ever known. Although she had never quite thought of Mrs. Hillary as a mother, she was still the only person Ursula could turn to. As she inched along, Ursula fondly recalled the many talks with Mrs. Hillary about Ursula one day coming back to Brookings to teach. Mrs. Hillary had told her that when the time came she would make the necessary arrangements for her to enter a teaching college in England. Strange, Ursula thought; she had never considered herself an orphan, yet she knew she was just as much an orphan as Clarissa, who was stumbling forward just ahead of her. "All right," she said to herself. "I am an orphan, but I'm going to make something of my life. I'm going to be a teacher."

Coming up the eastern side of the Piz Bernina, Peter stopped to get his bearings. He was dressed in his old alpine gear and had his skis strapped across his pack. Directly ahead of him was the Bernina glacier; Heidi and her friends would be coming from the southern side, and Peter knew from experience that the southern approach was the most dangerous. God, he thought, if anything happened to Heidi. . . . Peter quickened his pace, his long strides eating up the ground. Thinking of Heidi brought back the moment when he had put her in the cart at Dörfli for her journey to Italy. She was no longer a little girl. He had felt it then, and the feeling was even stronger now.

The sun was setting over the Alm as Mrs. Hillary made her way toward Grandfather's hut, which she could now see in the distance. She was somewhat apprehensive of how Grandfather would receive her, but she would have to deal with that as it happened. It had been a long day, and she was exhausted. The long walk up the Alm hadn't helped, but there were no taxis. She smiled at the recollection of the fuss the villagers in Dörfli had made over her car. They had never seen an automobile before and were very much in awe of this horseless machine. As she neared the hut she could see Grandfather, or a man she presumed to be Grandfather, cutting wood in the yard. Mrs. Hillary waved.

Grandfather looked up when he saw Mrs. Hillary approaching. From her appearance, he knew who she was. He struggled with himself to curtail the resentment he felt for Mrs. Hillary. He couldn't help but blame her for the entire fiasco.

"Hello! Are they here?" Mrs. Hillary said breathlessly. Grandfather shook his head and answered somewhat gruffly, "I have sent Peter after them." He pointed south toward the Piz Bernina glowing in the sunset. "They will be coming from there. Peter will find them, Mrs. Hillary. Now, you are cold and tired. I will make us some coffee and we will talk." In awe of this imposing man, Mrs. Hillary followed Grandfather into the hut.

Signor Bonelli had reached the edge of the glacier. Taking his binoculars, he carefully searched the southern face of the glacier and was immediately rewarded. He was able to make out the figures of children only two or three miles away and the fact that they were traveling very slowly. Smiling as he lowered the binoculars, Bonelli knew he had won. He could cover that distance in no more than two hours, and could easily afford the luxury of making a night camp. He smacked his lips at the thought of a decent meal, realizing that all he had eaten since he had started the search was chocolate. As the sun set, he scanned the horizon one last time. A frown appeared on his face, for coming from the north were dark cumulus clouds, the telltale sign of an approaching storm.

Halfway across the glacier, Heidi spotted the storm clouds at the same time Signor Bonelli did. Her alpine experience told her that she and her companions had at best an hour before the storm hit. They would have to find shelter and quickly. Adding to their problem, Heidi knew, was the fact that it would be dark within half an hour. The rest of the girls caught up with Heidi, and she pointed to the storm clouds.

"We don't have much time before it hits. We'll have to hurry."

The girls had by this time learned not to question Heidi's judgment. They knew their very survival depended on her.

"Let's go!" Ursula exclaimed.

In the Alm hut, Grandfather, measuring his words, looked across the wooden table at Mrs. Hillary, who was sipping her coffee. A comfortable fire burned in the stone fireplace.

"I have been trying not to blame you," Grandfather managed to say.

Mrs. Hillary set her cup down. "You're welcome to; I certainly blame myself. Not that it changes anything." Mrs. Hillary was bitter and very frustrated. Here the two of them sat, and there was not a thing they could do concerning the fate of the girls. "Sometimes I think the world has just gone out of control."

Grandfather considered this, and slowly shook his head. "The world was never in control. You would know that if you had ever lost a child."

"I lose every child I teach! In they come, and out they go! We barely have a chance to know them." Mrs. Hillary tightened her grip on her coffee cup. "It's even wrong to say I teach them. I don't."

Immediate recognition was etched on Grandfather's face, much to Mrs. Hillary's surprise. "They've taught you, haven't they?" Grandfather said quietly. Mrs. Hillary nodded, thinking, "He does understand; what an interesting man. No wonder Heidi always kept referring to her Grandfather and his wisdom."

"Yes, Heidi is a good example," she said aloud. "At first, I attempted to create the perfect Brookings girl in your granddaughter, but failed to see or understand that Heidi's basic strength and goodness, which came from you and all this, was her most important asset. I know better now."

Grandfather lighted his pipe with great care, making certain the tobacco was packed just right. He never expected someone like Mrs. Hillary, a headmistress of a fancy private school, to admit that she had been wrong and there were values other than deportment to be taught. He admitted to himself that he probably had misjudged her. When his pipe was drawing well, Grandfather got up from his chair and put another log on the fire.

"We both have learned something from Heidi," Grandfather said with his back to Mrs. Hillary.

"How so?" Mrs. Hillary asked. Satisfied that his fire was going well, Grandfather turned to face his guest. He thought for a moment before answering.

"When she first came to me, I had lost my wife, my

son, and I had turned my back on God and man and come up here to the Alm." He paused, searching for the right words. "I did not want Heidi, not at first. She was a burden to me. Her little voice was everywhere . . . questions constantly. I had no solitude, which I thought so important at the time. But it wasn't long before I came to understand that Heidi with her love was giving me far more than I gave her. She returned my life to me." Grandfather slowly walked back to the table and sat down in his favorite chair.

On the glacier the wind had picked up, a prelude to the fast approaching storm, as Heidi led her half-frozen band through the ice fields. Behind Heidi, separated by some ten feet each, were Ilsa, Clarissa, Gudron, and finally Ursula. Except for the moon's brief appearance through the storm clouds, it was now dark. Heidi knew there wasn't much time before the storm would hit with all its fury, but in the darkness it was nearly impossible for them to move at any speed. With the wind increasing, the ice seemed almost to moan, an eerie sound, high pitched and terrifying. As Heidi probed the ice ahead of her with the long pole, the moaning increased in intensity, building, building until a faint cracking sound somewhere in front of her brought Heidi to a complete stop. She instinctively knew something was very wrong. The moon reappeared for a brief moment, throwing its beam on the ice field and a towering shelf of ice before them that rose hundreds of feet. It seemed to Heidi to actually be swaying. She scrambled back to Ilsa and the others, waving to them to get down. Then, an explosive crack reverberated around them. Heidi looked up to see the face of the ice shelf begin to slide down the other side of the mountain—slowly at first, then faster and faster, until the avalanche was in full force, tumbling and crashing down the mountain. The girls could only stare in awe at the power of the avalanche, thankful that they had been spared. As the ice dust cleared, Heidi and the girls began to move slowly forward. The avalanche had sheared off the face of the mountain, leaving a giant cavern in the ice. It was as if the ice shelf had been hollow, thought Heidi. She moved quickly now, for the cavern was their salvation. The wind was howling, throwing its full force from the storm directly at the girls as they struggled onward. Heidi reached the cavern and breathed a sigh of relief, knowing they were safe. She helped the other girls to get deep within the ice cave.

Peter was caught in the full fury of the storm, but he kept going forward, hoping the avalanche had not taken Heidi and the other girls. He knew that if they were still alive they would have to be near the center of the avalanche. Snow began to fall, and the wind, which was now coming from the south, blew straight at Peter. He stopped to adjust his snow goggles. It was now impossible to see more than a few feet ahead.

Inside the ice cavern, the girls huddled around the small campfire Heidi had made from the pieces of wood the girls had carried in their packs. It had saved their lives, Ursula thought. Grateful for the fire's warmth, the girls slowly began to relax. Everyone realized how close they had come to being swept down the mountain by the avalanche. Gudron passed out some of the dried berries they had gathered their first day after leaving the battlefield.

"Will we get to Dörfli tomorrow?" Ilsa asked. Heidi accepted her ration of berries and considered Ilsa's question.

"It will depend on the storm. If there's not too much snow, we could be at Grandfather's this time tomorrow," Heidi said.

"Maybe we could build a sled," Clarissa added. Ilsa and Gudron giggled.

"Sure, we can make one out of ice, Clarissa." Gudron smirked. Ursula smiled; however, she was still thinking about what Heidi had said. "What will we do if there's heavy snow, Heidi?" she asked.

Heidi weighed the question carefully before answering. She did not want to alarm them, but she didn't want to give them false hopes either.

"It will depend on just how much snow. If we can make our way from here to the western rim, we should be all right. But it will take us a good day just to reach the rim, and another day, maybe less, to get down to Dörfli." Heidi studied her friends as they grasped the fact that they might have to spend another night on the glacier. At least they had some shelter in the ice cave. Heidi noticed Ilsa counting silently on her fingers.

"Ilsa, what are you counting?" Heidi asked. Ilsa looked at Heidi, then at the other girls.

"I just remembered . . . in twelve days it will be Christmas. We'll have Christmas in Dörfli!"

Ilsa's announcement that Christmas would be in twelve days stunned everyone. The ordeal of the past few days had completely obliterated any thought of the calendar. All but Heidi would be spending this joyous holiday in a new place, away from family and friends. Yet, Heidi knew they had all become very close since they had fled the orphanage, even Ursula, upon whom Heidi had come to depend more and more. With Grandfather and the girls, it would be a wonderful Christmas. Thinking of Grandfather, Heidi remembered the Advent poem he had taught her so many years ago.

"Advent, advent, a little light is burning. . . . first one, then two, then three, then four . . ." The other girls joined in. "Then next the Christ Child at the door." Clarissa crawled over to Heidi, who took her in her arms as Ursula began to sing "Oh, Holy Night." She had a beautiful voice, which echoed throughout the ice cavern.

Covered with snow from head to foot, Peter stood at the entrance to the cavern, listening to the Christmas hymn. Thank God, they were safe, Peter thought. He had almost given up hope until he had come across the cavern. Brushing himself off, Peter moved farther into the ice cave, guided by Ursula's lovely voice and the distant light from the girls' fire.

Gudron was the first one to spot what looked like the shadow of a giant as it moved through the cavern corridor toward their interior cave. She pointed and screamed, cutting Ursula off in midsong. Heidi immediately drew the army knife from her pack and stood to face the approaching terror. Ursula did the same, and stepped forward next to Heidi.

Peter had heard the scream, and realized his shadow had frightened the girls. "Heidi! It's me, Peter," he called out. Peter could see ahead of him the reflection of the girls' fire on the walls of the icy tunnel. Rounding a corner, Peter found himself in the ice cave facing Heidi.

Heidi had heard Peter call out. They all had. She had moved away from Ursula toward the cave entrance, but then had stopped. Peter, she thought. This is impossible. He's in the army. It must be some kind of trick. And she raised the knife in front of her. Even when Heidi saw Peter, standing at the entrance of the cave, she could not believe it.

"Heidi. It's me. Are you all right?" Peter asked quietly. The knife dropped from her hand. Heidi closed her eyes to clear the apparition before her, but on reopening them there he stood, and she was running to him. Peter took her in his strong arms and held her close.

The youngsters sat around the fire eating the army rations Peter had brought them. Never had any food tasted as good. There was no idle chatter; they just ate. After finishing their rations, Peter wanted to know the details of their journey. He looked to Heidi but she was strangely silent, so Ursula took up the story, followed by Gudron and Ilsa. Even Clarissa contributed to recounting their adventure. Peter was amazed, and realized that he had been very fortunate to find them. He put his arm around Heidi, who snuggled up close to him, completely at peace and relieved that Peter was there. He was there to take them down the mountain in the morning to Dörfli and Grandfather. Her last thoughts before drifting off to sleep were that she wouldn't have to be the leader anymore. Her wonderful Peter had come to her.

Peter threw the last log onto the fire. Heidi and the rest of the girls were sound asleep. As he held Heidi close, he worried about the next day. He knew the new snow was deep, too deep to take five girls safely down the mountain. There had already been one avalanche, and with the new snow the chances of another were very likely. He had to find another way.

CHAPTER 12

The sun rose quickly above the jagged peaks of the southern Alps, burning the morning mist off the Piz Bernina. Snow covered the glacier with a pristine white blanket that silenced the mountain against the usual northern winds. It was serenely quiet. Heidi and Peter stood at the cavern entrance, looking down at the puffy white clouds that had gathered at the foot of the glacier, giving the impression of a cotton-covered floor just below them.

"It's so beautiful," Heidi said, drawing in a deep breath of the cold air. She turned to Peter, who was already calculating the best route across the glacier to the western approach and his destination, the Swiss army's Bernina headquarters. He had sat up most of the night, and finally had made the decision to go for help. Peter had wakened Heidi and told her of his plan, but she had resisted the thought of his leaving her. In order not to wake the others, Peter had brought Heidi to the cavern's entrance, and it was only by force of logic that he had finally persuaded her. In order to get the girls safely across the glacier and down the mountain in the new snow, they needed help; wide snowshoes, poles for deep snow, and more rope, all of which were available at the Bernina outpost. Peter estimated that in the good weather he could reach the post in half a day and return before it got dark. They would start their journey to Dörfli the next morning.

"Well, I'd better get going. I left more food for you, but I'll bring back something special for tonight."

Heidi looked up into Peter's face. She knew what he was doing made sense, but now she was actually afraid to let him go. She pleaded. "Peter, let me go with you. Ursula can look after the girls . . . really."

Peter was tempted. It would be like the old days, just the two of them in the Alps. But common sense dictated the wiser course.

"Heidi, you've got to stay here. Ursula has never been in the mountains before. She wouldn't know what to do if anything happened."

"What's going to happen? I'll just tell her to keep everyone in the cave until we get back." Heidi had already made up her mind. Peter shook his head.

"Be sensible. You know better than most what can happen up here; and if it did, do you really want Ursula making those decisions?" Peter reached out and drew Heidi to him. "You know I'm right, don't you?" he asked.

Being in Peter's arms made her feel weak, even funny.

She mumbled a "yes" and knew she was feeling something wonderful. Peter pushed her hair away from her face. "I'll be back before you know it." He brushed her face with a kiss and was off.

With her hand to her face, Heidi watched Peter until he disappeared from view, then turned and entered the ice cavern.

After Heidi had told the girls of Peter's departure, she set them to repairing their packs and shoes in preparation for their journey down the mountain. She really only wanted to keep them busy until Peter returned. There was food to prepare left by Peter, and afterward Heidi planned to teach them the required technique for walking with snowshoes. All the girls were in good spirits, as they felt sure that Peter would see them safely down the mountain.

It was Ursula who saw him first. She couldn't believe her eyes. He was just standing at the cave entrance, smiling. His face was marked with red and blue frostbitten sores and his moustache was caked with ice. Ursula opened her mouth to scream, but nothing came out. Signor Bonelli, his reed-thin lips swollen and bleeding, let out a hideous cackle. "Finally!"

Clarissa screamed. "It's him!" Heidi pushed Clarissa behind her and picked up a heavy branch they were going to use for firewood, while Ursula, taking her cue from Heidi, found the knife in her pack. Gudron and Ilsa, both absolutely petrified, stood behind Ursula. Heidi was trembling with rage. How could this horror of a man have found them through the storm, she asked herself. This was impossible—tomorrow they would be in Dörfli. Heidi moved forward brandishing the branch, determined that Bonelli was not going to stop them. They had come too far.

Bonelli looked at this girl coming at him. He almost felt sorry for these little brats. But they knew too much and they would have to be silenced. His face burned with frostbite and his patience was exhausted.

"Who do you think you are? Did you think you could just run away? From me? I hate you and that idiotic Mrs. Hillary. I have waited years to get my hands on Brookings and you and your band of sewer rats aren't going to stop me."

Ursula was the first to reply. "You think you're going to get Brookings? You and that disgusting wife of yours wouldn't be trusted by decent people to collect their garbage, let alone their children."

Gudron added, "You are garbage." Being brave could be fun, she thought.

Clarissa wanted in on the insults. "And you have a creepy crawler on your face," she snapped, referring to Bonelli's frozen moustache and festering upper lip.

Heidi knew insults were not going to dissuade this man. She raised the branch. "We're not going back." She spat her next words: "Signor Bonelli."

There was not a lot of time. He wanted to do away with the girls and get back down the mountain. Enough is enough. Bonelli reached into his parka and withdrew a service revolver. He pointed the gun straight at Heidi and pulled the hammer into firing position. "Shut up or die here."

Heidi began to shake. He was serious. She looked over to Ursula. "Ursula, put the knife down. We'll have to go with him," she cried, dropping the piece of firewood.

Ursula was petrified. She threw the knife down and gathered the three younger girls around her. "Don't be afraid. We'll be all right."

Keeping the gun pointed at the girls, Bonelli moved in closer to Heidi. This was the one who had led them on their escape and caused all the problems for him and his wife. He trained the gun on the other girls and with his free hand slapped Heidi across the face, knocking her to the ground. He enjoyed it thoroughly. Bonelli pulled a rope from his pack and knelt beside her. He released the hammer and put the gun in his pocket. Keeping his eyes on the other girls, who stood motionless by the campfire, he tied Heidi's hands in front of her with the end of the rope. He pointed at little Clarissa and screeched, "You. Come here."

With tears in her eyes, Clarissa walked slowly toward Bonelli, knowing he would hit her too if she didn't obey. She began sobbing as Bonelli tied her hands with the same rope. One by one the other girls were tied to the rope, forming a chain with Bonelli at the head of the line and Heidi at the rear.

There was three feet of new snow on the ground from the storm. Heidi's wrists chafed against the coarse rope that pulled her and the other girls across the face of the mountain. Bonelli must be taking them back down to Tirano, where St. Mary's horror would welcome them again. The memory of the sewers and stench of the soap factory made Heidi's stomach turn. She looked at Clarissa ahead of her. A great lump rose in Heidi's throat when she thought of Clarissa never knowing anything but orphanages. The little girl had no parents or relatives, no one to care for her, and now she was returning to the worst place on earth. Heidi knew in her heart that she would get out when Mrs. Hillary or Grandfather finally arrived. But what about Clarissa?

Heidi refused to give up hope. She purposely began to walk as slowly as she could, pulling the group to a near crawl. She wasn't going to make this easier for Bonelli. Heidi tried to free her hands. Her wrists were bleeding from the strain. She continued to work the rope, trying to loosen it enough to get free. The ropes wouldn't move. "What would Peter do?" she thought. "Where is Peter?" She brought her hands to her mouth and gave the hawk call as loud as she could. If only he could hear her cry for help.

Peter found that negotiating the ice and rock while descending the glacier was just as dangerous as the climb up. Snow masked the craggy rocks, making it difficult to judge what was a safe foothold. What looked like a firm piece of snow-covered rock could turn out to be a thin piece of ice that would give way under any substantial weight. Peter tested his every step as he descended the western side of the Bernina glacier.

That Heidi and her friends had managed to get so far across the mountain amazed Peter. He knew what they were running from must be horrible, but to have the strength and determination to scale the Piz Bernina, some 13,300 feet high, was a formidable task for anyone. Surviving such high altitudes and severe weather conditions in mountainous terrain took more than good common sense. It took skills Peter had never realized Heidi possessed. Heidi had been his little friend since her arrival on the Alm when she was five years old. Now she was leading a band of young girls across one of Switzerland's most feared peaks. Grandfather had taught her to respect Nature's majestic rule, which man could never hope to conquer.

Peter was resting on a ledge and checking his gear when heard the call of a hawk. He looked up to find the bird but saw nothing. Again the hawk call echoed over the ice-shrouded mountain and again he saw no bird above him. As the sound reverberated around him, he listened carefully. It took Peter only a few more seconds to realize that no hawk would appear. It was Heidi's voice, far away. Why would she call, if not for help? Had Bonelli, against all odds, survived the storm and caught up with the girls? Peter wasn't going to wait to find out. Without a moment's hesitation, he packed his gear and turned around. He climbed the short distance of rock above him to reach a level surface where he could use his skis. Peter threw his pack down, untied the wooden skis and strapped them on. He couldn't see any sign of Heidi or her companions through his binoculars. Cursing himself for ever having left the girls alone, Peter shoved off with all his might in the direction of the hawk call and prayed nothing had happened to his friend.

Snow and ice ran beneath his skis at an intense speed. Peter maneuvered between exposed rock and snow with split-second timing. He could not waste time finding perfect open spaces. Crouching low with the ski poles clamped under his arms, Peter sped toward a small ledge. He could not see over it, but with no time to think, Peter catapulted off the ledge and into the air, leaning forward into the tips of his skis. A wide-open space exploded in front of him, the ground twenty feet below. He flew through the silent, frigid alpine air, knowing that if he broke from his stance he would tumble to the ground. The ground seemed to rise, slowly at first, as if he were floating down, and then there it was. Peter landed hard on the icy surface and, using every ounce of strength in his legs, turned to a stop. In front of him, the sheer, unobstructed face of the glacier dropped suddenly to a jagged edge. He gasped for air as he reached for his binoculars. Far in the distance, he spotted the girls being marched toward the glacier's edge.

"This is not the way down!" yelled Heidi.

"No. But it is a view everyone should see before they die!" Bonelli cackled.

Clarissa and Gudron screamed in horror. As they neared the edge, Heidi continued to work the ropes that were cutting into her wrists. She pulled at the length of rope in front of her to release some of the tension. Slowly, the ropes began to loosen. She looked ahead to Bonelli, who was dragging the rope closer and closer to the glacier's edge. Finally, she freed her hands, letting the others walk on. Heidi brought her hands to her mouth and gave the hawk call again. Bonelli whipped around to check the girls and saw Heidi several yards behind the group, looking up the mountain. He dropped the rope and ran toward Heidi.

"Heidi!" Ursula screamed. The girls scrambled to free themselves once Bonelli let go of the rope. Ursula and Gudron quickly untied themselves and tripped Bonelli as he ran for Heidi. Bonelli landed facedown in the snow, losing his grip on the revolver in his hand. He stood, pushed Ursula down, and started after Heidi.

Heidi saw something up the mountain, heading toward them very quickly. Could it be?

"Peter, Peter!" she screamed at the top of her voice. Bonelli was on her in a second, slapping her to the ground. Heidi kicked Bonelli hard in the shins and scrambled out of his reach.

"You'll pay!" Bonelli yelled.

Out of nowhere, Peter skied past the other girls, who only saw a blur whip by them. He slammed straight into Bonelli, sending them both rolling toward the glacier's edge. Peter could not stop himself. They were moving too fast.

Heidi looked on in horror. "No. Peter!" She could do nothing. The two men were feet away from the drop-off. Both rolled over the snowy ledge. Bonelli flew through the air. Peter caught hold of a rock jutting from the cliff. His head hit the rock, filling his vision with black spots. He looked down to see Bonelli's body smash against the rocks and land bloodied in the ravine a thousand feet below.

Heidi saw the two men roll off the cliff, not knowing which was which. She ran to the edge praying that a miracle had saved Peter. Please, God. When she saw Peter hanging on the edge, she burst into tears. He was alive!

"Heidi! Stop crying and get the rope," Peter yelled.

"Ursula, Ilsa, get the rope. Run!" she shrieked. "Hold on, Peter. Peter, don't let go. We'll pull you up. Don't move."

Ursula brought the rope and gave it to Heidi, who inched her way closer to Peter. She crawled on her stomach to the edge of the cliff and put the rope around Peter. She let her eyes wander to the drop below. No, don't look down, she said to herself. She passed the rope around Peter's chest and tied a bowline knot. Peter's arms ached with the strain.

"Pull! Pull!" she ordered. Slowly Peter pulled himself over the edge of the cliff. He lodged his feet against the rock he had held onto. It gave way and fell out from under him. Peter lunged for the ledge. He made it with his feet dangling over open air, and the girls pulled him to safety. He stood up, wiping the blood from his gashed forehead.

"Peter!" Heidi was sobbing as they embraced. The rest of the girls huddled around them. They were safe.

"Let's go home," said Peter.

CHAPTER 13

The old goatherd guided the last of his flock from the high pasture onto the well-packed trail that led to the valley and Dörfli below. He had labored most of the day at pulling his stranded goats from the deep snow drifts, and he knew he was most fortunate to have saved them all. The storm had brought the heaviest snowfall of the season. It would be nice for Christmas, the goatherd thought.

It was his custom before he began his journey down the mountain every day to give thanks to God for looking after him and his precious goats. Shielding his eyes against the brilliant sun, he looked up at the magnificent Piz Bernina rising several thousand feet above the Alm and muttered his usual prayer. He was about to turn to start after his goats when something caught his eye on the northern slope of the Piz. Could it be, he wondered. No, his sharp, old eyes had not betrayed him, for coming down the lower slope from the glacier were six figures, with what appeared to be a man in the lead. "It must be Peter with Heidi and the children," the goatherd said aloud. Offering another quick prayer of thanks, he hurried down the trail to signal the village.

With Peter in the lead, followed by Ursula, Gudron, Ilsa, Clarissa, and Heidi, the merry band traversed their way down the Piz Bernina on crude but effective snowshoes. Once they had crossed the remaining part of the glacier and reached the tree line, Peter had stopped to make all the necessary snowshoes out of the abundant fir trees.

Peter looked back to see how they were all doing and was pleased that they had just about mastered the technique of walking in the deep snow. Heidi, of course, had used snowshoes hundreds of times, At first it had been difficult for the other girls, particularly Ursula. She had fallen many times but had not complained once. What a change since that day on the edge of the glacier when Ursula confessed she had no parents. It now seemed like so long ago. Heidi vowed she would always be a close friend and do everything she could for her. The first thing she wanted to do when they got home was ask Grandfather to contact Mrs. Hillary. Heidi's thoughts of Ursula were interrupted when from across the valley of the Alm came the wail of a ram's horn. Someone had seen them. The sound echoed back and forth through the valley between the Alm and the Piz Bernina. They were almost there.

Farther down the Alm, the old goatherd raised his ram's horn to the sky and blew the rescuers' signal. It was answered by another shepherd nearer to Dörfli, and finally by someone in the valley, so that the sound reverberated back and forth between the two mountains.

In the Alm hut, Grandfather was putting the final touches to the Nativity scene; he had carved every piece himself. Mrs. Hillary took him the Advent wreath, which he put in its accustomed place in the window. As Grandfather lit the candles on the wreath, he heard the faint but unmistakable sound of the rams' horns. His hand shook. Could it be? He ran for the door, yelling to Mrs. Hillary to join him.

The sun was setting on the Alm as Peter, with Clarissa on his shoulders, made his way up the familiar trail. Ahead of him, Heidi was climbing the rocky path as fast as her legs would carry her, while Ursula, Gudron, and Ilsa were simply trying to keep up. Peter turned back to wave at the villagers who had come partway up the trail from Dörfli to wish them well. On hearing the rams' horns, several of the villagers had met Peter and the girls as they came down the mountain. They were given a ride in one of the villagers' straw-filled wagons. The old goatherd who had been the first to see them coming down the Piz Bernina handed out fresh bread and cheese, which were gratefully received by the girls. In response to Peter's wave, the goatherd once again put the ram's horn to his lips and signaled the successful return to Grandfather high up on the Alm.

Grandfather stood on the shelf of rock outside the hut and looked down the Alm toward Dörfli as the wonderful sound came again, drifting, echoing from peak to peak. Mrs. Hillary stood beside him, not knowing what to think. She pulled on Grandfather's arm. "What does it mean?" she asked. Grandfather turned to her, a smile on his face. "It means Peter has found them. They're coming home."

"Thank God!" exclaimed Mrs. Hillary, her eyes wet.

"Yes, thank God," echoed Grandfather. He turned his face skyward, and there was the Alm hawk, circling directly above him. "Bring them home, my friend. Bring them home," Grandfather whispered. The hawk gave a proud cry and then, with a flap of his mighty wings, the ancient predator headed southward toward the Piz Bernina.

When Heidi came into view she saw her grandfather and Mrs. Hillary above her and stopped, overcome with emotion, enabling the others to catch up. Heidi pointed out Mrs. Hillary to Ursula, who immediately began to cry. While Grandfather remained on the rocky shelf, giving his silent prayer of thanks for the return of his granddaughter, Mrs. Hillary, no longer able to restrain herself, tore down the narrow trail to Ursula, who ran to meet her. The two embraced. For Ursula, the ordeal was over.

As Ilsa and Gudron crowded around Mrs. Hillary and Ursula, Heidi took Peter's outstretched hand, and the two of them, with Clarissa still riding on Peter's shoulders, continued up the path to Grandfather. The old man realized that both youngsters had changed a great deal in the past few months, with Peter's experience in the army and Heidi's incredible journey. The two seemed very comfortable together. As they reached the rocky shelf, Heidi again saw her Grandfather standing there, and she ran into his outstretched arms. At last, Heidi was home.

Wiping her eyes, Heidi motioned for Peter and Clarissa to join them.

"This is Clarissa. She's from the orphanage," Heidi said. Peter put Clarissa down and she walked shyly toward Grandfather.

"You're Grandfather?" Clarissa asked. With a sweep of his still-powerful arm, Grandfather lifted her to his side. "I am Grandfather and from now on little one, for as long as you are here, I will look after you." Heidi knew her Grandfather was not an impulsive man, far from it. But today, whatever the reason, she understood only too well that an irrevocable bond had been formed between Grandfather and Clarissa. She was no longer an orphan. Still holding Clarissa, Grandfather extended his large hand to Peter. There were really no words that could express the gratitude he felt. And Peter, feeling Grandfather's strength in his hand and in his eyes, knew that at last he had been accepted as a man in his own right.

That night the girls sat around the stone fireplace recounting their adventures to Grandfather and Mrs. Hillary. They had been fed a wonderful supper of potato soup, fresh bread, and cheese, and were now warm and completely relaxed. Little Schwanli was very much taken with Clarissa and was curled up at her feet.

Peter had already taken his leave, to report back to his post in Sils Maria. Heidi was going with him as far as

Dörfli. After Ursula had told Mrs. Hillary and Grandfather of their trip through the orphanage sewer, the old man got up from his chair, visibly upset.

"Justice must be done, Mrs. Hillary. Saint Mary's must be shut down forever." Mrs. Hillary looked over at the girls, who were hanging on every word. She purposely did not want to involve them in this conversation.

"I agree and I have a plan, but let's first get these sleepyheads to bed. With the Christmas Eve pageant tomorrow, they're going to need all the sleep they can get."

Grandfather scooped Clarissa up, and turned to Gudron and Ilsa. "The three of you will sleep in Heidi's loft, Ursula down here with Mrs. Hillary, and Heidi will have my bed."

"But where will you sleep, Grandfather?" Clarissa asked him.

Still carrying Clarissa, Grandfather led the way up the stairs to the loft. "Ah, I will have the best bed of all. I will share with Schwanli a new bed of fresh straw I put down this morning." He carried Clarissa to the round window as Ilsa and Gudron jumped onto Heidi's straw bed so they also could see. It was a clear, beautiful night with the few lights of Dörfli twinkling below them. Grandfather couldn't help but think of the very first night so many years ago when he had held Heidi up to the round window. "You will have this window to look out on the Alm for as long as you wish, Clarissa," he said. Realizing what Grandfather was telling her, Clarissa reached up to his wonderful bearded face and gave him a kiss on the cheek.

"Grandfather, will you do me a favor?"

"If I can, my child," Grandfather replied.

"The boy we told you about, Giovanni; he's the one Signor Bonelli took back to the orphanage . . . ?" Grandfather remembered the children telling him about Bonelli and the dairy farm. "If it hadn't been for him, we wouldn't have gotten away. He's my friend and tomorrow I would like to light a Christmas candle for him. Is that all right?" Very moved, Grandfather could only nod his head.

Mrs. Hillary was making up Ursula's bed when Grandfather came down from the loft. "They're already sound asleep. Now, Mrs. Hillary, what are your plans?" Grandfather said. Mrs. Hillary looked over at Ursula, who was sitting on her bed, and motioned for her to join them.

"After the Christmas pageant tomorrow, Ursula and I will take Gudron and Ilsa to Zurich, where their parents will meet them." Mrs. Hillary put her arm around Ursula and gave her a slight hug. "Then the two of us will take the train to Lausanne, where we will take a large room overlooking the lake, and eat, sleep and enjoy the baths for a solid week."

"Oh, Mrs. Hillary!" Ursula exclaimed, deliriously happy. It would be just the two of them. Grandfather, however, cleared his throat. He didn't approve.

"I know, Grandfather. You want me to go immediately back to Tirano and speak to the authorities. We will, but not until after Lausanne. This child, whom I consider my own, has been through a terrible ordeal, as they all have. Rest assured, Ursula and I will be in Tirano in just over

144

a week's time. Besides the orphanage, I have a score to settle with that pompous governor, and believe me I shall." Grandfather couldn't help but smile.

"And what of Brookings?" he asked. Letting go of Ursula, Mrs. Hillary stood up straight.

"Grandfather, I will tell you that it will take more than a world war, an army, and a corrupt governor to keep me from getting my home back. Brookings is our life!"

Heidi and Peter stood in the shelter of a grove of tall pines, gazing at Dörfli just below. Every star in the heavens was out.

"Will you be able to come to the pageant?" Heidi asked Peter.

"I don't know, maybe. It will depend on my captain. I've already been gone a week. Do you want me to come?" Heidi laughed, and then put her head on Peter's shoulder.

"Yes, you idiot. I want you to come," she whispered. Peter lifted her chin and looked into her eyes. His only thought was that he had almost lost her, and he suddenly knew he never wanted them to be separated ever again. Bending his head, he kissed her gently on the lips. It seemed so natural; their bond was real and steadfast, rooted in friendship, and now another dimension had been added. Her knees were weak. Reaching up with both hands, she pulled Peter down to her and returned his kiss. Neither one spoke. Both were enjoying the euphoria, of the moment, attempting to grasp what had happened to them.

"I'd better go," Peter said haltingly. The last thing Heidi

wanted at that moment was for Peter to leave. She shook her head. "Heidi, I have to. . . . The army, remember?"

"Stay, and we'll watch the sun rise," said Heidi. "Please don't go, Peter." Peter kissed her once again, then gently put her arms down to her sides.

"I promise there will be many more sunrises, and sunsets, as long as you promise not to go running off again."

"I will if I want to," Heidi said gently.

"Then, I have to make sure you don't want to."

"Tomorrow?" asked Heidi.

"Tomorrow," Peter whispered. He brushed her lips with another kiss and ran down the trail toward Dörfli. Near the town wall, he turned and waved once, then was gone. Heidi looked up at the trillions of stars, wanting to sing out her happiness. This was her home, and she somehow knew that no matter what happened, it always would be . . . with Grandfather, and yes, definitely with Peter. Light-headed, she started back up her beloved Alm, and somewhere in the night she heard the distinct good-night call of the alpine hawk.